DARK DADAGIRI

HARLEEN MAKAR

Copyright © Harleen Makar 2025
All Rights Reserved.

ISBN
Paperback 979-8-89744-628-5
Hardcase 979-8-89929-966-7

This book has been published with all efforts taken to make the material error-free after the consent of the author. However, the author and the publisher do not assume and hereby disclaim any liability to any party for any loss, damage, or disruption caused by errors or omissions, whether such errors or omissions result from negligence, accident, or any other cause.

While every effort has been made to avoid any mistake or omission, this publication is being sold on the condition and understanding that neither the author nor the publishers or printers would be liable in any manner to any person by reason of any mistake or omission in this publication or for any action taken or omitted to be taken or advice rendered or accepted on the basis of this work. For any defect in printing or binding the publishers will be liable only to replace the defective copy by another copy of this work then available.

Contents

Preface

Dear readers,

I am elated that you are reading this book. Here is an interesting tale of how a corporate setup and a fast-paced environment affect the lives of young individuals.

Life is an adventurous journey, and the right perspective keeps it enjoyable throughout. The people who enter one's life in different phases greatly influence how it progresses. As situations change, one's status and relationships change, too. There can never be a solitary cause for such shifts; there are multiple reasons like lack of time, lack of patience, emotional weakness, etc. This story highlights the importance of trust, self-belief, and emotional strength in leading a joyous and balanced life amidst all the challenges.

The special poetic pieces at the end of each chapter highlight the take-home messages. I sincerely wish this read entertains you.

Happy reading!

Harleen Makar.

Acknowledgement

I am extremely grateful to my loving parents for their encouragement, guidance, and support in my writing endeavours.

Chapter 1

The Obvious and the Hidden

Alerted to an unusual and somewhat intimidating movement in the silence of the cold and dark night, Shivi rolled her eyes to the left and then cautiously turned her neck—just a bit—to check her surroundings. A few homeless men were sleeping on the sidewalk with their possessions tucked by their sides. Completely wrapped in patched blankets, they slept unbothered by the chirps of the crickets from the adjacent hedgerow. Above, there was a crazy swarm of flies hovering around the flickering streetlight. The muddy road behind didn't have any trace of footsteps either, reinforcing the absence of suspicious movement. The free end of Shivi's lightweight red cashmere shawl continued to wave in the chilly breeze, intermittently blocking her field of view. Pulling forth the sleeve of her sweater, she hid the delicate gold bracelet on her wrist. Turning back, she then paced forward faster.

Having moved barely a few steps from there, she felt as if a voice in her head said, *something does not feel right!*

Surrendering to this thought and the premonition, which she had had since that afternoon, she once again turned around to check. Astounded at the scene that unfurled in the distance, she screamed, "Sammy, move away!"

Dumping on the pavement the huge pile of shawls that she was carrying, Shivi sprang into action. In an elevated pitch, she repeated, "Sammy, move! He has a knife—the beggar has a knife!"

Her forceful tone echoed in the silence of the night, and the scary sounds of a fistfight followed. She sprinted down the street to help Sam as the fight between the men grew more intense. Reaching the spot, just as she was about to leap on the armed beggar from behind, another man appeared out of nowhere. Grabbing her left ankle, he pulled Shivi. Stunned by the forceful pull, Shivi fell face down onto the road. Her forehead missed the pavement by an inch.

Sam was terrified. He shouted, "Shivi, run to safety," and persevered in the hand-to-hand combat.

"No way!" replied Shivi.

Shivi's retaliatory kick took her assailant by surprise. Taken aback and hurt, the heavy-bodied miscreant fell onto the road.

Shivi's trim and lean appearance belied her self-defence abilities. Adequately trained to tackle such attacks, she immediately sounded the tiny, neon-yellow whistle hooked to her identity card. As a regular practice, Shivi never left for the field trips without her whistle, especially during night shifts. She also had the habit of carrying along a pepper spray bottle, which she had forgotten that day. Not that her job involved any particular risks, but she exercised caution at night.

In a matter of a few seconds, Shivi delivered another forceful knee kick. Then, she tied her assailant's hands behind his back using her shawl. Thus, neutralising him, she freed herself from his grasp. A few ladies who were sleeping by the roadside had also rushed to her rescue by then. They began scolding the culprit, whom they identified as a member of their clan. They also helped to restrain him and raised an alarm. A few men came running with bamboo sticks at their call and rushed to help Sam, who was still grappling with his assailant about twenty feet away.

Within a minute, two security guards arrived at the spot. Soon, the police also arrived and detained the two assailants. Sam and Shivi were to follow in order to file an official complaint.

Subsequently, Sam supported Shivi, his brave colleague and good friend, as she limped towards the office van. Inspecting her face, he said, "Shivi, your cheek looks badly bruised."

"Yes, it hurts. Thankfully, my head didn't hit the pavement. Otherwise, I'd have needed stitches. Since this afternoon, I had the intuition that something wasn't right. I feel this bracelet has a peculiarity. Whenever I wear it, I get into trouble."

She shook her arm to check but could not see the piece of jewellery. Immediately, turning around, she began looking for it. However, she could not find it anywhere on the road.

"What are you searching for?" asked Sam.

"My bracelet—I think it fell off during the fight. It was a gold bracelet. I can't afford to lose it. Turn on the torch, please!"

"Oh, no!"

Focusing the light onto the road, he also began looking for it.

When they could not find it, Sam said to her, "Shivi, we need to arrest the bleeding and disinfect your wounds. I'll come back to look for the bracelet. Let's get in the van and clean all this up first. There's a first aid kit in there. Then we also have to go to the police station."

"I know, but these wounds aren't hurting as much as losing my precious bracelet."

Half-heartedly, she proceeded towards the van.

Dark nights with stars twinkling in the sky, loads of relief materials in active young hands, swift movements, and conversations in whispers had always been the composing elements of the regular affairs of team *Seva Troop*, but such attacks were a rare occurrence—extremely rare.

Seva Troop was a humanitarian organisation that provided relief to communities in need nationwide. The headquarters of Seva Troop were at Connaught Place in Delhi. Their branch office was in East Delhi, and their field operations spanned the whole of India. From providing material relief to the masses during emergencies to year-round regular welfare activities for the underprivileged, this organisation undertook all related operations. A young, empathetic, and enthusiastic workforce formed the backbone of Seva Troop.

At a distance of about two kilometres from the crime scene, Dhaani, a tall and lean young girl, was at work. She was also a member of the Seva Troop team. Unaware of the brutal attack on her colleagues, she walked swiftly with a pile of blankets towards a group of ladies who were the newest occupants of the makeshift shelter under a flyover bridge. This shelter protected the homeless from seasonal extremes. Like many others in Delhi, this shelter too had occupants from the nomadic community—homeless, jobless families surviving on charity and alms from commuters. More often, these groups comprised migrants from other states who came to the city in search of jobs but ended up in shambles because of a lack of livelihood options. Surprisingly, these shelters eventually became their permanent residence until eviction—and that rarely happened. The plight of the kids and the toddlers—semi-clad, unkempt, crawling around, crying from hunger—often led their mothers to resort to begging. Risking their lives, these ladies braved the harsh weather just to receive the lowest denominations of currency as help when they urged the people sitting in cars that halted at the traffic signals.

To add to the woes of these families, there were leaders of the begging gangs who claimed control over the localised groups of beggars. These so-called leaders ruthlessly charged commission from the beggars. Threatening the families with assault and dislodging, they would exercise self-assumed territorial supremacy. During the daytime, it wasn't a rare sight to see little kids knocking on the windows of cars, eager to receive candy or, for that matter, just a coin. For them, getting a chocolate amounted to a windfall!

On reaching the spot, Dhaani approached two ladies who were cooking rice on a small stove by the roadside. She said to them, "It's almost midnight, and you are preparing food. You haven't eaten until now! Here, wrap these around your children," and handed them a blanket each.

Their kids got excited to feel the furry silkiness of their new companions for the impending chillier nights. Soon, they began cuddling in the blankets inside their tarps. The wide smiles on their faces were a testimony to the fact that sufficient protection from the chill was indeed a luxury for the underprivileged.

A little girl approached Dhaani from behind. She wore a ragged brown frock and oversized black slippers. Tugging at Dhaani's arm with her tiny hands, she said, "Aunty, I'm hungry. My mother is also hungry. We haven't had our meal today. My mother could not earn money, as she is sick." She pointed towards her mother, who lay on the pavement with a toddler by her side. Then the child added, "Are you going to provide us with food? Please give us some food."

Dhaani empathetically replied, "Oh dear! I'm afraid it's only blankets that we're distributing today."

While replying, Dhaani began searching the pockets of her grey-coloured tweed coat. The little girl eagerly fixed her eyes on Dhaani's wrist as she dug into the depths. Those eyes gleamed as Dhaani pulled out a couple of chocolates and handed them to the child. Dhaani said to her, "You can take these. I'll get some food for you people." The little girl was ecstatic to receive the treats and excitedly ran to show the bounty to her mother.

Suddenly, a deep voice echoed, "Dhaani, get in the van. The boss has ordered to halt the operations for tonight."

This was Vivaan's call. Vivaan was her friend and colleague. He had worriedly shouted from a distance while swiftly walking towards the office van.

"Halted! Why is it so?" asked Dhaani.

"Can you get in the van, please? I'll explain that later."

"Okay ... okay. Give me a minute, Vivaan. I'll just distribute these blankets and come. Can you hand me my tiffin from the van, please? They need food here."

"Okay, I'll get it. But Dhaani, please make it fast. We have to rush. A warning is flashing on the pager."

"Oh, mine ran out of battery!"

Dhaani completed her task. She also gave food to the child and hurriedly boarded the van. The driver was ready to jet off as his pager was buzzing, too. Vivaan and Dhaani were soon *en route* to the office of Seva Troop at Connaught Place.

Precisely adjusting the rear-view mirror, the driver told the duo, "There has been an untoward incident nearby."

Vivaan, who sat next to the driver, asked, "What happened?" Simultaneously, he took off his gloves and unwrapped his muffler as the brisk walk had made him sweat.

"I don't have any details yet, but there's been a tussle."

Sitting in the back seat, Dhaani concernedly stared into her phone. Next, she exclaimed, "Oh my God! Someone attacked Shivi!"

"What? Is she alright? Where is she?" asked Vivaan.

"Yes, she's heading to the police station with Sam. She just texted me."

"It must have been something serious," said Vivaan.

The driver, who was keenly listening to the conversation, joined in and contemplatively said, "Oh, that's why tonight's drive had to be stopped midway. Vivaan sir, I've been working with this company for so many years. Strangely, a similar freak incident happened last year. Otherwise, the distribution goes on smoothly till the wee hours in the winter months."

"This is so scary!" said Dhaani.

Within a few minutes, they reached the office. Dhaani and Vivaan began unloading the piles of shawls and blankets to submit them back into the storeroom. Minutes later, four more members of their team returned to the office in another van. However, even an hour from then, Shivi and Sam were nowhere to be seen. All the team members were clueless and terrified. Sitting outside on the bench in the garden, they anxiously awaited information about their colleagues. The heat from the coffee mugs that each of them held in their hands countered the effect of the chilly weather but couldn't allay the chill that stemmed from the slowly unfolding suspense.

A shining black sedan then pulled into the porch. It belonged to Ranjan, their team leader.

Vivaan thought, *Shivi and Sam haven't returned, and Ranjan hasn't given us any information either! Where is he going? Is he homebound?*

He enquired of the office boy, "Is Ranjan sir leaving for the day? Did he say anything about Sam and Shivi?"

"No, Ranjan sir has received a call from the police station. He's heading there," the office boy replied.

"Oh, okay," said Vivaan.

Seeing Ranjan exit the office building, Dhaani ran towards him and spoke with him in the middle of the driveway.

She hastily asked, "Excuse me, sir. Do you have any information about Shivi and Sam? I hope they are alright!"

"Yes, young lady! Your colleagues are fine. All of you can leave for the day. The guard has locked the storeroom. Hopefully, we'll resume the distribution day after tomorrow."

"Right, sir. But do you have any idea when they will return?"

A devious smile appeared on his face, and he replied, "Gorgeous girl, I have to complete some formalities at the police station before your beloved colleagues can return. Don't take too much stress; it'll destroy your beautiful skin."

Dhaani was a twenty-three-year-old girl from the hills of Himachal. She was undoubtedly the perfect specimen of natural beauty; however, Ranjan's style of addressing had more to do with his lecherous intent.

Smashing a cigarette butt under the heel of his tan-coloured ankle boots, he walked away in his signature, mischievous gait. This man's body language rarely gave away anything about him. Lighting another cigarette and blowing away the smoke, seemingly unbothered, he then sat in the back seat of his car and left. A chain smoker, Ranjan blatantly ignored the multiple prohibitive signboards at the office, which warned about the injurious effects of active and passive smoking. He was more of a nuisance in power at the office!

Subsequently, about an hour later, all the formalities were completed at the police station. As soon as all three of them came out of the building, Ranjan authoritatively instructed Sam, "Help Shivi sit in the front seat of my car. I've sent the van back to the office as the driver got an emergency call and had to go home. I'll drop both of you on my way back."

"It'll be a long ride for you, sir. My hostel doesn't even come on your route. I'll take an auto rickshaw and shall also drop Shivi home," Sam replied.

Lighting a cigarette, Ranjan walked away to his car while saying, "You can do whatever suits you, young lad. But Shivi is definitely going in my car."

Hearing this, Shivi clutched Sam's hand quite hard, giving him a piece of her mind and gestured for him to accompany both of them. She obviously didn't want to be left alone with Ranjan. Sam was also quite angry at Ranjan but had to eat his own words. In a forced about-turn, he said, "No, actually, you are right, sir. It's almost midnight and even I won't be able to find a ride. I'll be grateful if you drop me home too," and he moved forth, suppressing his anger.

Soon, they embarked on the return journey. A little later, they reached the housing complex where Shivi stayed as a paying guest. One of her roommates was already at the gate to receive her, as she needed assistance to walk.

The men had barely driven half a kilometre when Ranjan told Sam, "There's not enough petrol in the tank for the car to go the extra distance to your residence, so you'll have to get down here and walk to your destination. I'll be taking the shortcut to my place."

I knew it, thought Sam. He immediately said, "No issues, sir," and opened the door to get out. Half-heartedly yet politely, he added, "Thanks, sir. Good night."

As soon as he began walking, he texted Shivi and asked if she had settled. She, in turn, enquired if he had returned home. They got on a call the next moment, and Sam asked, "What makes you think that Ranjan would have taken pains to give me a lift to my place?"

"What are you saying, Sammy? Don't tell me he left you midway?"

"Yes, he just wanted to drop you off, Ms. Shivi Singh! I've told you so many times to be cautious with this rogue."

"I know that, and I'm always very careful. It was you who was going to leave me alone with him today."

"Yes, I apologise for that. What I actually meant was that I would drop you at your home, but he is such a sharp man. How audaciously he wanted to take advantage of the situation!"

"Actually, it's nobody's fault. Today was just a bad day. I feel miserable. I also lost my bracelet during the tussle. My mom had gifted it to me this year on my birthday."

"I'm sorry for your loss. I'll surely go there and check tomorrow morning before going to the office. Maybe I can find it."

"I'd be grateful if you could do that for me. I'm unable to walk properly, so I'm taking a day off from the office tomorrow."

"Yes, you need to rest. I'm also entering the gate of my hostel now. I'll catch up with you in the morning. Bye."

They then ended the call.

Shivi Singh was a psychology graduate from the University of Delhi and joined Seva Troop a year ago, while Sam Fernandes was a public health graduate. He hailed from Tamil Nadu and had been working with this company for the last four years. Both had become great friends right from the day Shivi joined the office, as she had initially trained under Sam. In informal settings, she fondly addressed him as *Sammy*.

Right from the beginning, Sam appreciated the dedication with which Shivi approached her work. Impressed by her skills, he had even recommended her name to the top management for a sponsored executive MBA right after her training. However, Ranjan had voted against the proposal and advanced the candidature of one of his favourites for the same. Ranjan had his own group of conniving assistants. Year after year, he selectively hired undeserving candidates from campus interviews, often overlooking the team's recommendations; not hiring meritorious ones was his trend. After merely three to six months of training, most of them were fired. The ones who survived beyond this timeframe either agreed and adapted to his vile methods or surrendered to his wishes owing to the dire need to be employed—they couldn't afford to quit their very first job.

Back at the office, the next day, Ranjan called Sam to his cabin and said, "Sam, I am entrusting you with the responsibility of running quality checks on a consignment of edible relief materials from a company in Gujarat." After a pause, he added, "This is a very important project, and it will give you ample exposure in a new area of Seva Troop's operations. I am purposely staying out of it so you can get a novel experience."

Subsequently, they had a brief discussion.

On first impression, Sam doubted Ranjan's intention. He thought, *Ranjan is up to some mischief again. Edible relief materials are not my responsibility. He always handles them himself. In the last managerial meeting, when I requested a diversification in my duties, he outrightly put down my request. I can't understand why he is sending me to Gujarat for this now. I'm sure he hasn't had a change of heart, so I'll have to figure out what his intention is.*

While exiting the cabin, Sam bumped hard into the glass door, owing to the confusion in his mind. However, he regained composure almost immediately. The thoughts lingered in his mind even as he dutifully carried out the day's work.

At the end of the exceptionally busy day, Sam called up Shivi to enquire about her health. During the conversation, Shivi said, "You know what? Ranjan called me up in the afternoon and informed me that I need to go to the branch office in Chandigarh for a training programme in the coming week."

"Really? What training is it? He didn't even wait for you to be well and back on duty. I'm surprised at this."

"Yes, even I was surprised. He wanted me to complete the registration formalities ASAP and said that he'd book the tickets after the call. He sounded rather aggressive. However, I firmly reiterated that I'll only be going if I'm fit to travel."

"How did he react to that?"

"Suddenly, he feigned compassion and said that he thought I'd be up and about by now."

"It isn't strange at all for a person like him to do that! No one knows what goes on in his mind."

After the call, while working out in the gym, several doubts arose in his mind. Sam thought, *Ranjan has ordered me to go to Gujarat and wants Shivi to go to Chandigarh—but why Shivi—when she just went through a terrible ordeal yesterday? He could have picked Dhaani for this training. He isn't allowing Shivi a breather. For the last two years, I've been on the team that takes charge of the operations in Chandigarh. I'm unconvinced about this change. I'm sure he plans to accompany Shivi to Chandigarh. This man is up to something!*

Meanwhile, at midnight, when they connected, he kept his doubts to himself. Thoughtful enough, he didn't speak his mind. Instead, he just told Shivi to get some rest. She had already opted out of field operations for a week because of the sprain in her ankle. Therefore, he knew she was safe from Ranjan's trap until then.

There's a variety of shades

Of human nature out there:

From the cosy and warm

To the sly and deceptive!

And deciphering is a whole big maze,

Not a simple or rosy affair.

Chapter 2

Leads and Deliberations

A couple of days later, it was business as usual for Dhaani and Vivaan as they boarded the office van around 8:00 p.m., along with two of their co-workers. That night, the load of relief materials was less. Only the leftover blankets and shawls from the last lot were to be distributed. Other than those, they were to distribute freshly cooked food and dry ration items in one of the slum areas that a raging fire had hit three days back. The fire gutted about a hundred jhuggis, leaving affected families in the lurch. An NGO had approached Seva Troop to help with relief operations in that slum.

While on their way to the slum, Dhaani told Vivaan, "The raw materials are already at the site and so are the cooks. I guess it's just going to be a two-hour affair."

"Yes, you're right. It shouldn't take longer than that. We should be back before midnight."

"I remember that the last time we went for such a distribution, there was utter chaos at the site."

"Yes, the one at Jangpura! I remember being pinched and punched throughout the distribution. Actually, the plight of the slum dwellers makes them desperate. It's not their fault."

Soon, they reached the site, and the operations began. The distribution drive progressed well except for tugging at the site because of the desperation of the slum dwellers to procure food. Dhaani accidentally even poured a ladleful of hot porridge over her own hand while serving. For a moment, there was a commotion, but Vivaan gave her first aid immediately, and she felt better. Despite this, there was a lightness in everyone's mood—the fun part being that nobody seemed bothered about her injury, and all just carried on with their hustle! Seeing this, Dhaani also forgot her pain. They were back at the headquarters at around 11:00 p.m.

While they were leaving for the day, Sam asked Vivaan, "So, what are your plans for the next two days? I'm sure you're not trading this time off for sleep!"

"No plans at all! Dhaani wants to get some rest. I'm also tired. We've had an unusually packed week. I pity you, though."

"Well, I don't have any option but to go to Gujarat for this assignment, which Ranjan has forced on me. I'll take compensatory leave next week and combine it with the weekend to visit my mother."

"I think Dhaani plans to spend some time with Shivi tomorrow."

"No, Shivi won't be here. I talked to her last night. Her sprain has almost healed. She has taken another two days off and is going to visit her parents at her native place in Himachal Pradesh. Actually, she wanted to skip the programme at Chandigarh because she wanted to avoid travelling the distance with Ranjan. So, she's heading home tomorrow."

"Oh, really? I must inform Dhaani then. I'll send her a text. Maybe she'll go shopping with me tomorrow."

They bade goodbye and headed home.

The next day, Sam dropped Shivi off at the railway station and then headed to Gujarat. She boarded the train for Shimla. Upon reaching Shimla, she took a connecting ride to her village, Kalpa, which is in the Kinnaur district of Himachal Pradesh.

The sunrise had brought along quite a breezy morning in the Sutlej River valley. Now at her home, Shivi had a slight backache and was running a fever too. However, for her, it was pretty normal to have such health issues post-travelling. So, ignoring the aches and donning winter gear, she headed out for her yoga session amidst the natural serenity with her younger sister, Sargam. Sargam was a bright ninth grader. She looked exactly like Shivi—sharp features, black eyes, straight brown hair, and a fair complexion; however, her traits weren't like Shivi's.

Sargam always looked forward to this enjoyable time with her elder sister because she could venture out to the open areas in the hills with her. While they were walking towards their destination, briskly navigating through the tortuous roads, Sargam candidly said to Shivi, "You know what? A family here wants you to get married to their eldest son. They own an apple orchard here and are pretty well-off. They had asked Mummy and Papa."

"What? Mummy didn't mention anything to me. When did this happen?"

"Perhaps because Mummy has rejected their offer."

"Thank God she did! I'm in no mood for marriage at present."

"I know, but they are still pressuring Mummy and Papa. The day before yesterday, the Sarpanch Uncle came to our house. I was in my room. I heard him bring up the topic once again with Papa."

Shivi became concerned, but she didn't want her little sister to feel insecure, so she said, "Sargam, don't worry. I'm sure our parents can handle this. Their liberal thinking makes all the difference. They allowed me to pursue my higher studies in the city. Most of my friends here didn't even get that chance."

"Yes, and Mummy says that they'll send me to Delhi too so that I can pursue high school studies in a metropolitan city. She believes it gives the much-needed exposure."

"Of course, by the time you come there, I'll have settled down in my job and shall be able to provide for you."

They hugged each other. The shine of a bright future was evident on Sargam's face. However, Shivi became concerned about the sensitive issue mentioned by Sargam. She couldn't help centring her thoughts there.

In the evening, Shivi got busy helping her mother with the kitchen chores. Her father came home and brought some friends along. Shivi prepared tea for all of them while her mother took charge of preparing snacks.

At the tea table, one of Shivi's father's friends asked him about his plans to get Shivi married. Her father casually avoided answering, but she could see that the faces of her parents reflected awkwardness. Shivi wanted to ask her mother about the family, which was unduly pressuring them. At night, she talked to her mother, who immediately set her mind at rest, reassuring her that she needn't worry about it. She said, "We shall handle everything. Darling, you just focus on spending a good time here and go back with a free mind. We sent you to the city because we wanted you to make a good life and a secure future for yourself. We don't want to get you married here in the community because then you'd have to settle in the village eventually. If you can, you must work towards a better life. You can achieve that by making the city your home."

Shivi hugged her mother and said, "Mummy, you can just say I am not interested in getting married so soon. That way, they won't have a reason to pester you."

"No, we won't be able to brush it aside like that because this is a village, and the culture here differs from the cities. The family's reputation here and their might may lead the community to boycott us. They might force us to move out. We can't afford to be ostracised. This is our home. Your father and I are just sticking to the narrative that you are going to appear for a crucial exam soon, and we can't disturb you at this point in time."

"Wow, that's an intelligent excuse, Mummy!"

"Okay, now you must sleep. It's late."

"Can I sleep in your arms for a while? I miss you so much in Delhi."

"Sure, my child ... come."

She then slept comfortably, enjoying the soft pats from her mother.

The next morning, they all went to visit their spiritual guru at a temple, which was a few kilometres from their village. All that Shivi prayed for that day was the well-being of her family and a favourable solution to the issue at hand.

Time passed swiftly. Soon Shivi was back at work in Delhi and had joined her co-workers in the field operations. Shivi and Dhaani were good friends. Shivi requested Ranjan to send Dhaani with her for the distribution drive, as Sam still hadn't returned from Gujarat. Ranjan acceded to this request of hers. His nasty intentions and hidden desires to please young girls overpowered his duties as a boss, at times. That night, the girls finally got to discuss the incident that had happened a week back. Dhaani asked Shivi, "Did the police call you again for anything—I mean, did they record your statement?"

"No, I haven't received a call from them. The inspector on duty was a thorough gentleman, though. He could see that I was concerned for my safety and had assured me I needn't worry. In fact, I was thinking of asking Ranjan if he received any updates, but then Sammy told me to wait until he returns from Gujarat. You know how Ranjan is— things can get very uncomfortable."

"I can very well understand. Ranjan is a shady personality. A step here or there, and one might fall into his trap! I don't know why the management does nothing about it—I mean, most of the female employees feel the same about the environment at our workplace."

"See, the thing is that all of us are fairly new employees. Perhaps that's the reason no one wants to risk their job. It all boils down to the fact that it's we—the girls—who aren't feeling comfortable. No one has any solid issue, reason, or even proof on which to base the grievance. He doesn't leave any pawprints! We just have to be on guard to avoid mishaps."

"Yes, I just hope that no girl ever falls into his trap. Maybe it's the same everywhere; if not, just the degree of intrusiveness may vary from workplace to workplace. Let's talk about something positive now. How was your trip home?"

"It was good. My parents are doing fine. Sargam is excited to come to Delhi for her high school next year. She told me to shortlist schools for her!"

"That sounds great. So, you'll have a lot of big sister duties to do once she arrives."

While they were talking, they came across a child who asked Dhaani, "Aunty, do you have any chocolates today?"

Realising that it was the same child whom she had earlier met, she picked the child up in her arms and cuddled her. Then, she told the child, "Not chocolates, but I do have something special for you."

Pulling out a tiny bottle of orange juice from her sling bag, she smiled and gave it to her. The child was very happy to receive it. Such cute moments were definitely the highlights of the day for the young and active workforce at Seva Troop. Later, they returned home after their duty was over.

Since Seva Troop primarily worked to provide aid and relief materials to the underprivileged, they often had to work night shifts in the winter months. The next day, Sam returned and joined Shivi for another night-time distribution drive in a slum in East Delhi.

Shivi asked Sam, "How was your experience at Dairy Good Food in Gujarat? Were you able to complete the task successfully? Why didn't Ranjan go this time?"

"That's exactly the question which remains unanswered! I haven't been able to figure out why he sent me. It was he whose presence would have worked. I had to sign all the papers on his behalf. I even took help from a manager in the company there because Ranjan was supposed to oversee the quality check, which I did not know. The situation was a total mess."

"Really? It must have been embarrassing for you!"

"Yes, it was! And intriguingly, the training programme in Chandigarh also got cancelled at the last moment. Neither did anyone see Ranjan in the office, nor was he on leave. The cherry on top is that no one can question him—he is our boss!"

Both had a good laugh and continued with the distribution drive.

A couple of days later, Ranjan and Sam had a major face-off at the office. It so happened that there was a mismatch in the quantity of materials in the consignment, which was sent by Dairy Good Food. The quantity was just fifty percent of the promised amount. A high-level meeting was called to discuss the issue at hand.

When asked about the details, Ranjan put all the blame on Sam. He said, "I suspect gross misdoings on Sam's part." Ranjan's audacity in the presence of the treasurers and founders left Sam dumbstruck. Sam countered, "Ranjan assigned me the job at the last minute, and I didn't even have the required information to complete the task."

During the heated discussion, Ranjan accused Sam of paying more attention to Shivi than to his work. Now, Ranjan was hitting below the belt, and Sam couldn't tolerate it. Infuriated, he replied in the same coin. He asked, "Do you think I am like you?"

Soon, the altercation turned into a shouting match. The security guards had to be called to bring both men under control as Ranjan tried to attack Sam by laying his hands on Sam's collar. Both were given strict warnings by the management, and an inquiry was ordered.

Sam was pretty stressed by the sequence of events that had unfolded. Consequently, he felt demotivated at work. Unfortunately, the office politics intensified and reached a deplorable level. Everyone except Ranjan and his close aides felt uncomfortable. Blame games day in and day out dampened the mood of the workforce. However, the virtuous motto of their organisation pushed all employees to do their best each day.

Some days later, at the same flyover bridge where they had been attacked, Sam and Shivi were distributing food packets when a beggar walked up to Sam. He asked Sam, "If I'm not wrong, it was you whom two beggars had attacked here some days ago?"

Sam replied, "Sharp memory! Yes, you're right."

"Sir, do you have any information about the men who attacked you? Although they came back the next morning …"

Sam interrupted, "Wait, what? How did they come back the next morning? We had filed a complaint, and they were in the police's custody."

"Sir, I don't know how, but they did return. And that very evening, they had an altercation with a tall, dark, robust man. Afterwards, they went somewhere with that person in his luxurious car. Although the two men returned the next day, a week ago, someone came during the night and again took them away in a car. They haven't returned since then."

Shivi asked, "Did they escape punishment?"

"I don't know about that," answered the beggar.

Sam gestured to Shivi not to react too much. He told the man that he had no information about them. Then they proceeded further with their work.

A day later, Sam went to the police station to check with the investigating officer and found out that someone had withdrawn the complaint on behalf of Seva Troop the morning following the attack. This information came as a shock. Subsequently, Sam and Shivi resolved to ask the management about it. After all, the safety of employees is paramount, and they deserved to know the details.

There is a lot to be seen beyond the obvious;

There can be hidden truths,

There can be hidden intentions,

There can be malicious thoughts,

And also a breach of trust.

Chapter 3

More Food for Thought

Time flew by. It was now the month of August, and autumn was approaching. Seva Troop had been entrusted with another responsibility, and that was to set up an emergency relief camp for pilgrims who were stuck on their way to the Badrinath temple in Uttarakhand. Tremendous rains had hit the area, and unfortunately, landslides followed, bringing the pilgrimage plans of devotees to a scary halt.

Upon reaching the heart of the impact zone, members of the humanitarian convoy began their operations. Distressed travellers looking for food, clothing, and hygiene essentials were queuing up, hoping for some relief. The team dedicatedly and empathetically began serving them all.

While stacking the hygiene kits on the table, Shivi said to Dhaani, "Thankfully, there have not been many casualties, but there's a persistent fear of more landslides and boulders rolling uncontrolled because of the incessant heavy downpour. It is scary, isn't it?"

"Absolutely. The local inhabitants have also been advised to stay indoors, and the disaster response teams have evacuated the susceptible areas," Dhaani replied.

The team members at the adjacent table handed over food packets to the pilgrims. Next on their list of duties was catering to the need for a supply of edible raw materials to the people holed up in their homes. The men from the team took on the responsibility; they directed the women to stay back at the camp, as the uneven terrain intensified the danger.

Later in the night, by the campfire, this bunch of young workers of Seva Troop sat and chatted to allay the unease from the day's stress. While pondering over the reasons for such anger that nature shows in the form of catastrophes, Shivi said to Dhaani, "It was a tough day. As we sit here warming ourselves, there are still so many people on this mountain stretch who need help and are waiting for it. Apart from pilgrims, the locals also face these troubles annually. I wish we had more hands and more daytime hours to serve them all. However, there's one thing that I'm grateful for—God kept Ranjan away from this drive! It would have been so awkward otherwise."

"Absolutely! Carrying on with our duties in this restricted space and with limited means would have been a nightmare in his presence. He wouldn't have left a single chance to ogle and overstep all boundaries."

"Dhaani, I forgot to tell you something!"

"What? Go ahead."

"Sammy learnt that someone withdrew the complaint against our attackers. He was furious about it and is going to bring it up in the next meeting with the management."

"What are you saying?"

While they were talking, the men's team returned. Sam seemed to be in a hurry. He grabbed a stool, sat next to Shivi and said irately, "I told you he was up to something!"

Shivi wasn't expecting any news here, so she calmly asked, "Who is up to what, Sammy? You had gone for relief work. Was there a hitch there? Why are you so red with anger?"

"Ranjan, of course... who else? Today, on our way back, I was having a casual chat with the driver, and the topic of that attack came up. He told me that Ranjan had visited the police station the very next day after the attack."

Dhaani leaned towards them out of curiosity.

Sam added, "I am sure Ranjan was the one who withdrew the complaint. He didn't even come to the office the next day. This corroborates his involvement."

"Oh, yes—the driver is absolutely right. I recollect that at the office, we received a couple of calls from the police station that afternoon, asking for Ranjan," intervened Dhaani.

"He also told me that Ranjan had visible injury marks when he returned to the office a day later. His elbows had bruises, and he had a sore neck. He looked off balance and smoked heavily the whole day. Even the fire alarm went off that day at the office. When the driver asked him about his bruises, he said that he had a scuffle with someone over a parking space at his residence."

"What are you trying to say, Sammy? I'm getting confused," said Shivi.

"Shivi, remember a beggar near the flyover told you the other day that the attackers had an altercation with someone after returning from the police station?"

"Yes, I do remember," replied Shivi.

Dhaani was aghast, and she asked, "Oh, are you trying to say that there can be a connection between your attackers and Ranjan?"

"Exactly. Ranjan was untraceable for a day. When he reappeared, he looked injured, and so were the miscreants," replied Sam.

Shivi was clueless, so she asked Sam, "But why would Ranjan have picked a fight with them? We've believed until now that he was the one who got them released! Correct me if I'm wrong."

Dhaani exclaimed, "Oh my God! That's exactly the point—getting them released—there can be a connection! Shivi, there's definitely something fishy. Sam's doubt isn't unreasonable."

Both Dhaani and Sam then explained their suspicion to Shivi, who eventually got their point. Sam vowed to get to the depth of the issue once they were back in Delhi. He affirmatively said, "I won't let Ranjan brush things under the carpet. He will have to answer. I swear, if I find out that he had anything to do with that attack on both of us, he'll be in big trouble. I'll bring it up in the next weekly meeting."

"But you mustn't do that in Ranjan's presence. The last time, that crazy man turned to violence—remember that board meeting?"

Tempers were high, and keeping calm was tough. However, they all settled into their sleeping bags to get some rest. The next day, they had to go several kilometres further to set up another relief camp.

Amidst the fear of impending heavy rainfall and the scare of landslides, these young people from Seva Troop were a ray of hope for the public. They had to heat food packets and distribute them among the villagers. They also had to hand out tarpaulins, blankets, and clothing essentials to the residents. Three days later, the relief operation ended with a sense of contentment as the team saw smiles on the faces of the pilgrims and the inhabitants of the village. The frenzy had ended, and they all felt secure.

Back in Delhi, the workload was very light. The weather was pleasant, and there were still a couple of months to go before the chill would set in. It was more of a cyclical work for the team. The team members had to do night shifts during the winter. During peak summers, their job revolved around providing amenities at community shelters set up to protect the underprivileged from the heatwave during the daytime.

Three months passed by pretty quickly. On this day, Shivi and Sam were again in the vicinity of the same flyover, distributing warm fortified milk to needy children in a slum. Small kids queued up to grab chocolate milk on a windy night. Their eyes gleamed at the sight of the tall glasses of milk, and the colourful straws fascinated them. It was a sight to behold—a scene that could sow the seeds of benevolence in any soul.

Dhaani and Vivaan were handing over packets of biscuits, while Shivi and Sam were distributing the milk. There was tea for the elders. For the slum dwellers, it was no less than a treat. Everyone seemed to enjoy the warm drinks, and some kids even returned to ask for more milk. Interestingly, the colours of the glasses fascinated them more than the milk! After about an hour, the distribution came to a close, and they all began wrapping up. Just then, Dhaani remembered a place nearby and said, "Oh, I've heard there's a pastry shop here. College students often hang out there. My flatmates were raving about it one day."

"Let's check it out. As it is, I'm hungry," said Vivaan.

So, the four youngsters planned to grab coffee and some sandwiches for themselves before leaving. They told the driver that they'd be back in ten minutes. Subsequently, they returned with steaming hot coffee and grilled cheese sandwiches. They waited to consume the food in the van while on their way back. The driver ate his sandwich rather quickly—before beginning the ride.

Biting into the gooey cheese sandwich, Shivi admiringly said, "Mmm ... this is heavenly."

"Right, and this coffee is heavenly too," added Dhaani.

The men nodded in appreciation.

Sam said, "So, it was the last operation for the season. Apart from one odd night, the drive went so smoothly. It really is a blessing to help these homeless people as a part of our job."

"Seeing the satisfaction on the faces of the adults and the excitement on the faces of little kids is so heartening," added Vivaan.

The girls echoed, "Certainly!" and high-fived.

The driver murmured something and then went silent. Noticing this, Sam asked him, "Did you say something?"

"Umm ... yes! While you were away, something strange happened."

"What happened?"

"A lady came to me and began talking about the unfortunate attack on you and Shivi Madam. She belonged to that clan. Actually, she had seen our van pass by the T-junction, and she came to enquire where the distribution was going on."

"Really?" asked Sam. He instantly added, "I wish we had some reserves in the van that you could have given to her."

"Yes, even I thought so. I guided her to the slum where the distribution was going on. However, she stayed and then began talking. She told me that those two men have been missing for a few days. They just disappeared in the night a couple of days back. She seemed disturbed and said that their wives and children are worried. She added that this is the third time they've gone missing!"

Sam frowned and said, "This sounds strange." For a few moments, he seemed lost in thought. The girls in the back seat expressed concern, but Sam gestured for them to stay silent as he didn't want them to say anything in the presence of the driver. Soon, they reached the office, where they had a brief yet intense discussion, after which all of them headed home.

The following week, they all had to head to Bangalore for a celebratory event organised by the founders of Seva Troop. It was a three-day affair that included discussions on the achievements of the company in the last year, setting new targets, the announcement of promotions, and many engaging activities for the employees. The highlight for this group of four friends was that Sam had been cleared of the charges of misconduct levelled against him by Ranjan in the edible relief materials case relating to the company, Dairy Good Food. The company in Gujarat had found one of its employees guilty of siphoning off relief materials for commission. They then passed on the information to the investigating committee. Seva Troop promoted Sam, and with the higher role, they offered him enhanced compensation. They applauded him for his continuing valuable contribution.

Sam expressed gratitude and elation; however, he held onto the suspicion that Ranjan had something to do with this case, too. He was very sure that Ranjan had manipulated things in order to avoid being named. However, he didn't have the time or resources to get to the depth of this issue, so he let it go.

Subsequent to the role appraisal, Sam now held the same position as Ranjan—both were now managers but were heading two separate arms of the relief programmes. As a subordinate, Sam had earlier kept mum on a number of occasions. However, now his position gave him the freedom to speak out and bring to light Ranjan's misdoings. As expected, things began becoming even more troublesome at the Delhi office.

A few months passed, and it was time for an audit. This time, Sam was actively involved in it because of the higher role that had been given to him. Marred by organisational politics, rush, and confusion, it turned out to be a bittersweet experience. However, Sam was relieved that the audit concluded in the stipulated time, and he delivered his duties well.

On the following weekend, the four friends met for lunch. Their talk revolved mostly around the revelatory aspects of the audit. Sam began discussing it. He excitedly said, "On the second day of the audit, the auditors found a major mismatch of figures. Accounts were checked, and it became known that Ranjan had withdrawn noticeable sums of money twice and siphoned it all off as cash withdrawals. Answers were sought from him, and all his efforts to justify the withdrawals went to waste. He could not give concrete replies to the auditors. I keenly observed all the happenings."

Shivi intervened and said, "Sammy, your excitement tells me you've got some evidence against him ... isn't it?"

Sam replied, "Not evidence, but I got some leads. The time of those withdrawals strangely coincided with the month in which we were attacked. The first thought that came to my mind was that this is where we could find concrete evidence against Ranjan to support the correlation between the two incidents."

"But this won't lead you anywhere. You know Ranjan very well. He doesn't leave any traces of his misdoings," said Shivi.

"I know that, Shivi. Perhaps I'm overthinking. However, I'm going to follow my gut feeling and shall continue to look for evidence against him."

Dhaani and Vivaan soon began talking about the food, and then the topic shifted to lighter talk about new movies. They had an enjoyable afternoon, after which they went to watch a movie impromptu. They ended the day by indulging in their favourite ice cream sundae, for which all four friends had a shared liking.

Sam was an undeniably intelligent chap. One night, he visited that flyover again. He wasn't expecting to meet the miscreants because the driver had already mentioned them being missing, but he was hoping to get a lead. Wanting to connect the dots, he took the chance. He approached an old lady who had also taken shelter like others there at the traffic signal. She was communicative and seemed somewhat familiar. He talked to her for a while. She recognised him, as he had been there several times for the relief material distribution drives. Showing her a picture on the phone, he asked if she recognised the man in the picture. She could not confirm if she had seen that man earlier. It was Ranjan's picture, and Sam was desperately looking for a lead. She called a couple of ladies from her community, but they also couldn't help. Unfortunately, Sam returned empty-handed. However, true to his detective-like nature, he didn't leave it at that. For the next few weeks, he vigilantly drove by the spot to see if those men had returned. But he did not succeed.

One day, he approached the old lady again, took her into confidence, and convinced her to help him with the issue. He requested her to seek information from the wives of those attackers about any inflow of sizeable sums of money. In turn, he offered monetary help to her, which she refused. So, to compensate for her effort, he began giving her home-cooked food every other night. Eventually, she told him to stop doing so, as people from her clan were suspecting his intentions.

She gathered every bit of information that she could, intending to get back to him on one of his visits. One day, she told him to meet her near an old banyan tree down the road. He waited at the spot. She came and, wasting no time, said, "I have some important information for you. I have been told that one day, both men brought thirty thousand rupees each. They handed over the money to their wives, who then travelled to the village to keep the money safe there. But this was a long time back."

Sam knew at that moment that he had struck gold!

He enquired, "Did they tell you precisely when this happened?"

"I asked them about it. They couldn't tell me the dates, but they told me it was around Kartik Purnima."

"Kartik Purnima," he said and added after a contemplative pause, "Thank you for your help." He then gave her some money in return for the favour she had done. Upon returning home, the first thing he did was to find the precise date of Kartik Purnima. He then came to know that there was a difference of a week between the cash withdrawal from the company and the men getting the money. However, he still lacked proof to corroborate his theory. Unfortunately, there was nothing more he could think of to get to the root of the plot at this point in time.

The churning of thoughts

Leads to meaningful extractions.

Be it at an instant or at a later time,

The mist does clear up—the mist of distractions.

Chapter 4

The Emergency Call

Sam was the only son of his parents. His mother used to live in Nagpur with her sister-in-law. Both ladies lost their husbands to a car accident years ago. Sam was just sixteen years old when his father passed away. His mother had been a stay-at-home parent until then. However, because of responsibilities, she began working and continued to do so until Sam got his first job. When Sam got settled in his job, he took up the responsibility of running the house. It was then that he assured her she didn't need to worry about running the house. His paternal aunt lived with her, and both ladies were thick friends since Sam's parents got married. When Sam moved to Delhi, both ladies began staying together. His aunt was a teacher by profession.

One day, Sam got an emergency call from his mother. His mother seemed low, and she said, "Sam, I have developed a gastrointestinal issue. I am having difficulty in digesting food, and heartburn troubles me a lot. My appetite has dropped. I consulted our family physician. He prescribed medicines for a week, but I didn't get any relief, so he referred me to a specialist. Now, the specialist has prescribed so many tests. Your aunt is also unwell. Her knees are giving her a tough time. I'm unable to manage all of this alone. Can you come here for a couple of days and help us with these medical chores?"

"Of course, Mom. I'll take a few days off from work. I'll be there with you tomorrow. Please don't worry. Let me inform my boss, and I'll get back to you."

As soon as their call was over, Mrs Fernandes put down the phone and gave her sister-in-law a big smile of accomplishment!

The very next day, Sam arrived in Nagpur. Seeing his mother and aunt sitting on their front lawn and giggling away while sipping coffee, he was perplexed. He walked towards them and said, "Hello, beautiful ladies!"

Both the ladies got up and gave him a tight hug—a group hug. He said, "I'm glad to see you smiling. I was so worried for both of you. Especially, Mom's gastric issue gave me jitters, knowing that she had a similar problem five years back." He pulled a chair, made himself comfortable, and, looking at the table, exclaimed, "You are having pizza and cake! Mom, you shouldn't be eating this—it'll get you in trouble." His tone had subtle yet noticeable notes of anger.

His mom pinched his cheeks, and his aunt playfully fluffed his hair while saying, "Haha, we tricked you!"

His mother candidly said to him, "Sam, we have a surprise for you."

"What's the surprise, Mom?"

"For a long time, we've been wanting a daughter-in-law, and God has been kind enough to send a prospective bride for you without us even looking for one. We have a family from our friend circle visiting us today. Their daughter seems to be the perfect match for you. That's what we both feel, and that's why we called you here!"

Sam interrupted, "Mom, I've been so busy with work and still, I took days off and rushed home—not for this—no way, Mom! You've been planning and plotting behind my back. This is so unfair."

He dejectedly got up from the chair and nodded his head. Although they expected such a reaction from Sam, the tone in which he expressed his disappointment upset the ladies.

His aunt sternly said, "Sam, we want to get you married, and this girl is a gem of a person. We've already met her parents. We didn't want to lose this chance. There wasn't any other option. If we had told you, you would have refused. Correct me if I'm wrong."

Sam responded, "You aren't wrong. I wouldn't have come to this meeting." His voice had notes of helplessness in it. He added, "But I have reasons for refusing. I need to be settled and must have a good financial standing before I get married. I need a couple of more years to accomplish that. The last time Mummy had asked me about it, I had expressed my thoughts clearly. It was just two months ago, if I'm not wrong."

His mother held her hands to her forehead and sank into the chair in despair. Her pulled-down eyebrows and raised upper lip clearly reflected her anger. Witnessing her reaction, Sam realised that now there was no escape for him. He couldn't have explained or convinced them—he didn't stand a chance.

In the evening, the girl's family came over for tea. They brought along Rose, their daughter. Rose wore a peach-coloured, calf-length dress paired with delicate shimmer sandals. The brown-eyed girl had shoulder-length hair with golden highlights and wore a beautiful satin bow in her hair. Well-groomed from top to toe, she looked very attractive indeed. A few inches shorter than Sam, but just as lean as him, she paired very well with him. This was a perfect match by the looks of it. She was three years younger than him and had just begun working at an MNC. Customary greetings gave way to warm conversations about the families from each side. The dainty-looking girl just looked up at Sam interestingly, as if wanting to convey her feelings. His mother noticed that and told both to go to the lawn and talk freely.

When they came back after fifteen minutes, the elders had finished their tea, and it was time for the guests to head back. Neither Sam nor Rose conveyed any decision to their respective families, although both had exchanged phone numbers. As they said goodbye, their pleasing smiles temporarily allayed Sam's mother's fear of indecision.

At the dinner table that day, his mother asked him, "Sam, how did you like Rose? Have you decided anything? The girl's family must be waiting to know your decision."

"Mom, what decision are you talking about? We just met and talked for a few minutes. You wanted me to meet her, and I did just that!"

"Don't overreact. By decision, I just mean to ask what I should say if they call me up?"

"Well, Rose is a nice girl, and I enjoyed talking to her. She didn't seem very interested in a fast-tracked marriage. I could understand that her side of the story is the same as mine. But we've exchanged numbers. Maybe we can meet again next time when I come here. There's nothing more to it."

"This generation, I tell you! Is this a game, or what? We are looking forward to getting the children married, and these youngsters are on their own journey of taking it easy and being friends."

"Mom, don't worry so much. I'm sure she isn't saying yes anytime soon. So, you won't get a call from her parents. To be honest, I actually explained to her that she needs to tell her parents about her wishes instead of meeting prospective matches under pressure."

"Thank you, Mr. Counsellor!" exclaimed his mother in a sarcastic tone.

"It's not about counselling, Mom. She is young, and sometimes girls find it tough to express clearly to their parents about what they actually feel. I know a couple of such cases that happened at my office. Young girls marry under parental pressure, and they end up dissatisfied with their lives. One of my juniors is currently going through a bitter divorce, and she's just twenty-one!"

Sam's mother had nothing more to say. Perhaps she felt that Sam needed some time too.

A couple of days later, he was back at the office in Delhi. During the lunch break, he was chatting with Shivi when she asked him, "Sammy, how's Mrs. Fernandes doing now?"

"Oh, she's doing fine."

"I'm relieved to hear that ... and how's your aunt? What about the doctor's visits? Is everything settled now?"

"No doctor visits, no illness—it was pure blackmail," said Sam.

"What? Why are you saying that, Sammy?"

"They tricked me!"

"Are you serious? Your mom missed you so much that she feigned illness! I can't believe that."

Shivi had just asked this and burst into laughter when Dhaani and Vivaan also joined them in the cafeteria. Dhaani came and sat next to Shivi. Vivaan high-fived Sam and sat next to him.

"Guys, the fragrance of Rasam is wafting through the air and tickling my taste buds! Why don't you have any food on your plates?" asked Vivaan.

"Vivaan, we just came in five minutes ago," replied Sam.

"Let's go get some food," said Shivi as she held Dhaani's hand and got up from her chair.

She winked at Dhaani and whispered to her, "Come, let me tell you something. Sammy's mom is fine. She pretended to be sick and called him to meet her in Nagpur." Dhaani also broke out laughing, and both walked towards the buffet spread. The men chatted for a minute and then followed the girls to the buffet table. Their chit-chat continued while they got food for themselves.

Back at the table, while relishing the food, Dhaani teasingly said to Sam, "I got to know that your mom tricked you! Maybe you should plan trips home more often."

"Yes, she did! She gave me a big surprise too."

"Aww ... that sounds so nice. Tell us more about it."

"Hmm ... not nice. She and my aunt plan to get me married. It was a plot to make me meet a girl whom they liked."

Hearing this, Dhaani exclaimed, "Wow! Really?"

Shivi smiled too, but her eyes didn't quite seem to support her facial reaction. She looked somewhat shocked. She exclaimed, "What!" There wasn't a word more from her. Perhaps she was confused.

When lunch was over, Dhaani and Vivaan returned to their desks while Shivi excused herself for the day by simply saying, "I'm not feeling very well. I'll be heading home."

The day progressed as usual at the office. Sam checked on Shivi in the evening through a message, to which she didn't promptly reply. Then Dhaani called her up and found out that she had been sleeping through the afternoon and was feeling better now. Later that night, they all met again to celebrate Vivaan's birthday, and he cut the cake when the clock struck twelve. Sam then drove

Shivi back to her home. She was largely quiet that night. Sam himself began talking about Rose. He explained how awkward he had felt when his mom sent him and Rose to talk privately. Then, he shared how he broke the ice and made Rose understand that she needed to be more assertive in such matters.

Some questions were arising in Shivi's mind—about Sam, about Rose, and about their future—but she didn't say a word. She listened to him patiently. Perhaps she was having a hard time suppressing her emotions. Perhaps she was tired and also eager to reach her destination. Successful at guarding her mental state, she got out of the car at her society's gate and bade him a calm goodbye despite the turmoil inside her.

The next day, she told Dhaani she'd be going out for a walk during lunchtime, as she wasn't feeling hungry. Dhaani instantly reminded her of the lunch plan and said, "It is Vivaan's birthday today. Even if you don't want to eat, you can at least be with all of us. He's also treating the entire team to an ice cream party after lunch."

"I completely forgot about it. I'll be there for the celebration."

"Why don't you take some fresh lime soda? You'll feel better."

"I already had it, but it didn't relieve my nausea. Maybe the mango shake I consumed at the market two days ago didn't suit me."

"Do you have a stomach ache too?"

"No, I'm just feeling bloated."

"You must go to a physician if it doesn't settle today."

"Yes, I also thought so."

Over the next few days, Dhaani noticed Shivi wasn't her chirpy self—she wasn't talking much—not even to Sam. Sam asked her what the issue was, but she herself wasn't able to figure it out. A couple of times, she snapped at Sam without any reason and then regretted her behaviour. On some days, she was ecstatic and talked her heart out to him. On other days, she went totally silent. A sea change was noticeable in Shivi's activities. She preferred alone time as opposed to outings with friends. She even took a week off from work and visited her parents.

Sam's personal life was where all the activity was taking place. At times, he felt overwhelmed, as things were happening at a fast pace. He talked to Rose more often. His mother was happy about it and looked forward to having Rose as her daughter-in-law. He used to share these developments with Shivi, as with Dhaani and Vivaan. Subtle changes were developing in his camaraderie with Shivi contemporarily. His time was now divided between Rose and Shivi. Perhaps this was the reason Shivi felt left out. However, neither did she complain to him, nor did she ever broach the issue.

Sensitivity proves that

Feelings control human nature.

From developing a soul connection—

To disinterest—to indifference—

What one does with these feelings

Actually controls the future.

Chapter 5

It's All About Shivi

Things were progressing quickly, and two months later, Sam headed to Nagpur again. He met Rose. It looked like he was getting along well with her. The families were happy to see some progress on this front.

One evening, the young duo met at a cafeteria, and Rose candidly said to Sam, "You were so right! Out of fear, I never told my parents that I needed more time before I get married. When I talked to them, they instantly agreed. They appreciated your maturity when I told them I got this advice from you."

"I'm happy to hear this, Rose. So, this means we are now meeting as friends!"

"Yes, friends presently. But it would be a lie if I said that I'm not looking at the prospect of marrying a person like you."

"Wow, boss lady! You are awesome. So clear with your thought process. I don't know about the future, but I'm glad I found a friend in you."

"I'm glad too. Your presence has brought a sea change in my thinking. I feel free; I feel liberated—no pressure at all!"

"Mom wanted to meet you, Rose. She told me to convey her message to you."

"Yes, sure. Even I wish to see her. I haven't met her in a while. Sometimes it's work, sometimes family, and sometimes friends that keep me busy. However, I'll pay her a visit soon. You must give her my regards."

"Sure, I will. You could even call her up and talk if you can't take time out to meet her. She'll feel good."

"Oh, yes. I'll do that."

Then Rose's phone rang. It was a call from her office, and she had to leave for some work. Their meeting ended on a beautiful note, and both were looking forward to seeing each other again. After spending a day at home with his mother and aunt, Sam headed back to Delhi.

Six months zoomed by. Things went smoothly on the work front, too. Vivaan and Dhaani had simultaneously begun preparing for the civil services examination. It was going to be the first attempt for both of them. They joined a coaching centre where they went for classes on the weekends. So, they no longer had time to spare for the weekend outings, which had been a regular feature with the four friends earlier. Shivi and Sam were mostly free on weekends, so Sam often made plans to watch movies at a cineplex on Sunday evenings with Shivi.

On one such outing, Shivi wanted to leave the movie halfway and insisted on returning home. Sam said to her, "If you're not finding it interesting, let's go back. I'll drop you at your home."

"No, you continue watching the movie. It's a nice one, but I'm just not feeling well. I'll take an auto rickshaw and go home."

"No, Shivi. I'm coming with you. Wait!"

"No, please."

She said this and left the hall in a jiffy. He got up and went behind her, but she swiftly made her way out, and before he could spot her, she was gone.

He thought, *Shivi is behaving strangely. Did I make her uncomfortable? It was a nice science-fiction movie. Why did she leave it halfway?*

Sam felt uncomfortable and didn't want to go back to the hall, so he grabbed a sandwich and planned to return home. In the meantime, Shivi texted him, saying that he must watch the movie. She warned him that if he didn't, she would get angry with him.

After reading her message, he thought, *this girl ... she is so unpredictable. I better complete the movie now!*

The next day, during lunchtime, Sam talked about it to Dhaani, who agreed with his thought that something wasn't normal with Shivi. Dhaani said, "I can see that she backs out at the last moment and avoids outings. I'm unable to figure out why she feels unsettled. Often, she skips having food with us too. Today also, she's not here!"

"I've asked her if it has something to do with her family back in Himachal Pradesh, but she denied that. Actually, she isn't accepting that there is something which is not normal. She used to chat comfortably at length with me earlier. Now, she avoids looking me in the eye sometimes."

"She is mostly busy talking on the phone. Her frequency of calling home has doubled. I hope all is well there. Don't worry, Sam. I think I'll skip my class this weekend and spend time with her. We need to get to the root of this."

"Yes, that sounds right. Thanks for helping me with this, Dhaani."

The next weekend, Dhaani informed Shivi that she was going to spend Sunday with her. Shivi welcomed her decision. They cooked a hearty meal and enjoyed a movie at Shivi's place. After watching the movie, Dhaani insisted on going out and having an ice cream. While at the ice cream parlour, Dhaani told Shivi, "Shivi, you know what? After so many days, I'm seeing the chirpy side of my friend once again! Maybe because I've been busy, you feel lonely, and that's why you've been feeling low."

"No, not at all, Dhaani. Don't think this way."

"Then what was it, Shivi? I want to know what was spoiling your mood—is everything okay back home?"

"Yes, all is well at home."

"Are you sure you have nothing to share?"

"There isn't anything that I'm hiding, believe me."

Dhaani held her hand and said, "I trust you completely. If you ever feel like sharing anything, don't hesitate. If I'm not near you, just know that I'm just a call away."

They hugged each other, and the evening ended on a very positive note.

The next day at the office, Sam excitedly went to Shivi's desk and showed her passes for the trade fair, which was going to begin in a couple of days. Over the past three years, they had been going together to the trade fair, as Shivi loved to shop there. Dhaani and Vivaan had opted out this year because of their coaching classes and busy schedules. Seeing the passes, Shivi shook her head and said to Sam, "I don't feel like going this time. Dhaani isn't going either."

Sam countered, "Shivi, enough of this attitude!"

He grabbed her hand and told her to come with him to the cafeteria. She followed him. They sat at a table, and a visibly irked Sam asked, "What is the matter? Earlier, you were so enthusiastic about outings. You never bothered whether it was you and me, or four, or even ten other people going with us. You just wanted to have fun and spend some quality time. What's going on, Shivi?"

Shivi became emotional. Sam's heart melted, and he instantly patted her head to comfort her. He said, "Shivi, our friendship was never like this. You were never so formal. Have I made a mistake? Please tell me so that I can rectify it."

Shivi just nodded; her heart was so full—she continued to weep. He got her some coffee. On regaining composure, she said, "I don't know what it is—I just don't know. The only thing I know is that I'm not happy—nothing has changed, but nothing feels the same either. I feel lost."

For a good five minutes, she cried—cried her heart out. Sam just kept comforting her so that she could let those emotions out.

"It's okay, Shivi. Take your time, my dear. If it's just an emotional phase that you are going through, your friends are there with you and will be there for you always. I'm the same Sam—your Sammy! You can count on me, and I mean it, Shivi."

Shivi felt better after the heart-to-heart talk, and she returned to work.

Subsequently, Sam's positivity rubbed off on Shivi once again, and they revived their joyous camaraderie. Slowly and gradually, fun made a re-entry into their hectic work schedules. Shivi became joyous once again, knowing that her friends had her back.

If they try to understand all that you leave unsaid,

If they try to take the burden off your chest,

If they can feel your emotions just by a touch,

They're precious and must be valued just as much.

Chapter 6

The Trip to Solan

A few months later, Sam and Shivi planned a weekend getaway to Solan for all four of them, as Dhaani and Vivaan direly needed a break from their studies. Although this place was six hours away from Shivi's home, she decided not to visit her family as time wouldn't permit.

It was Thursday evening, and Friday was an official holiday, so they set out on their journey on this evening itself. It was going to be a seven-hour drive. They had decided beforehand where they were going to stop for snacks and later for dinner. Sam had always been in charge of all such decisions. He was a foodie and loved travelling, so he was the most experienced within the group. All four were excited and looked forward to spending the weekend visiting the monasteries, temples, and enjoying nature's scenic beauty amidst the hilly embrace. Shivi was especially looking forward to visiting the Jatoli Shiv temple, which she had heard about from her mother since childhood but never had a chance to visit. She wished to experience the tranquillity.

On reaching Solan, they checked into a resort where they were going to stay for two days.

On Friday morning, Sam got a call from Rose. While talking, she casually mentioned that she was in

Chandigarh for a conference. This pleasantly surprised Sam. He proposed out of curiosity and said, "Seems like we can meet! I'm in Solan. I guess it's about a two-hour drive from your location. If you have some time, let's meet."

"Oh yes, that's a brilliant idea!"

"Listen, why don't you drive half the distance so we can meet somewhere midway for lunch?"

"I wish I could do that, Rose. However, my friends and I have plans for lunch already. I can't ditch them. It'd be great if you could come and join us here?"

"Sam, don't bother. This option just popped up in my head because I didn't want to lose an opportunity to spend time with you. I didn't mean to spoil your plan with your friends. You must continue with your plan."

"It's fine, Rose. I didn't take it that way either."

"By the way, you never mentioned this trip to me. You should have! Anyway, I know you like being with your friends. We can meet some other time."

"I thought I had mentioned it when we last talked. Maybe I forgot. However, suit yourself, Rose. If you change your mind, let me know. We'll be happy to have you join us."

Shivi overheard just this last bit of the conversation. When Sam ended the call, she asked him, "Sammy, what are you doing here? Who were you talking to? We've been waiting for you at the poolside. Is someone joining us?"

"It was Rose. She's around and wanted to meet me."

Just then, Dhaani also came looking for both of them. She exclaimed, "Guys, it's going to rain. So, we've got a table indoors in the Chinese restaurant. The Mughlai Hall is already full."

"Okay, let's go then," replied Sam, and all three of them went inside.

At the restaurant, there was a guitarist performing melodious romantic numbers. Dhaani was excited and asked Vivaan if he wanted to dance to the mesmerising tunes. Sam and Shivi cheered in agreement, and they both hit the floor. Grooving to the rhythm of classic tunes, they swayed perfectly. Flinging her arms around Vivaan, Dhaani playfully smiled as he made her whirl around. She swung, and he pulled her lovingly, tightening his grip on her hand. After an enjoyable dance, when they returned, Dhaani saw that Shivi was emotional. Dhaani thought, *Maybe Shivi needs a companion too. Her eyes reflect her loneliness. As far as I know, she doesn't have a love interest…I hope I haven't missed out on her life updates. Why did she become so emotional? Maybe something in the past left her heartbroken, and the shadow remains in her thoughts.*

While Sam told Vivaan about the call from Rose, Dhaani closely watched Shivi as if she had a doubt in her mind. Shivi's lost looks, her wistful gaze, her pursed lips, and the stance of her hands—all were telling a story—a deeper story.

The tunes from the guitar strings amply complemented the feisty lunch, and the mood of the afternoon was welcoming. The warm aroma of ginger emanating from the beautifully presented dishes was soothing enough to energise them for the six-day workweek ahead. This was a much-awaited vacation.

As they were ordering desserts, they got a surprise! Rose entered through the door of the hall. Sam got up from his chair as soon as he saw her. He exclaimed, "What a beautiful surprise!" He walked towards her. They held hands, hugged each other, and proceeded towards the table. He excitedly introduced her to his friends. All then sat down. Shivi moved closer to Dhaani and offered her place to Rose.

Rose said, "I took half a day off. I had to finish a lecture. I'm going to spend the evening with you all."

"Wow, that's great," commented Sam.

Dhaani and Vivaan seconded him. Shivi smiled. Dhaani was quick to notice the sudden change in Shivi's behaviour on Rose's arrival. They all chatted at length over the last course of desserts. Shivi joined the conversation only a couple of times, asking Rose some questions about her life. It was more of a formality. She seemed to have lost interest in the conversation. However, Rose answered happily. Soon, they left the restaurant and headed for a monastery visit. Later in the evening, Rose left for Chandigarh.

The next day, all four friends went to the Jatoli Shiv temple. Shivi was particularly excited about this visit. She had decked up in an ethnic ensemble and seemed full of reverence, ready to pay her obeisance and receive divine blessings. The visit was all about absorbing the divine vibes in the cleansing environment. Once they were done, they began driving back to the resort. The weather was breezy. Shivi and Sam had dozed off in the car. Dhaani and Vivaan stopped midway for a tea break. As they sat on a bench at a tea stall, Dhaani concernedly said to Vivaan, "I noticed something very peculiar yesterday."

"What was it? Was it about me? Did I impress you with one of my many traits?" asked Vivaan naughtily.

"Stop it! I'm talking about Shivi's behaviour."

"Shivi's behaviour?"

"Yes, when Rose surprised Sam, I noticed Shivi felt tremendous discomfort. It was visible in her body language."

"Oh, how did I miss that? Tell me more about it."

"Stop being mischievous. This is serious."

"Okay, my apologies. I am deeply concerned about Shivi's well-being. I was just teasing you."

"In the first place, Shivi wasn't happy to see Rose. She covered up by staying silent most of the time, but her questions to Rose were pointed—unreasonably pointed!"

"Oh yes, I recall that. She asked Rose about her marriage plans! I thought she was pulling her leg because Sam already told us that their plan was up in the air."

"Exactly, and then she asked Rose about her expectations from a life partner. Who asks that of a person whom one has just met? That question made the situation awkward for Rose."

"So, you're saying that Shivi was being mean to Rose on purpose?"

"Yes, and I feel she is getting insecure about Sam being in a relationship."

"Very much possible."

"But that's not fair. She has to be clear about her own intentions. Shivi and Sam are the best of friends, and we know that. However, she can't be ruining his chances of getting a decent partner."

"Dhaani, on the contrary, this sounds so interesting—Shivi and Sam in a relationship! You should be playing cupid instead of critically analysing Shivi's reactions. Girl, what are you doing?"

"You're misunderstanding me. I would be glad if Shivi and Sam came together. I'm just saying that given the present circumstances, her behaviour towards Rose wasn't justifiable."

"Talk to her. Perhaps she needs clarity for herself. Perhaps she needs some hand-holding."

"Yes, I'll talk to her, and that too soon."

Then they went back, sat in the car, and drove off. Back at the resort, they had brunch and left for some more sightseeing. On Sunday, they left Solan in the morning and headed to Karnal, their last destination en route to Delhi. They were to stay in Karnal until the evening.

It was about two in the afternoon when they went to Karna Lake to enjoy boating. Afterwards, they went to the local market. While roaming in the lanes flanked by carts of street hawkers, Sam got excited to see a lady decorating dupattas with colourful motifs. He approached her and asked about her craft. On being told that these were vegetable dyes, he requested her to create a dupatta for his mother in her favourite colour, which was green. Sam's halt at the place attracted Dhaani's attention, and she followed, taking Shivi along. Sam excitedly told the girls that he had ordered a dupatta. Before he could elaborate, Shivi said to him, "Okay! So, Rose's favourite colour is green."

"What made you think that I'm getting this for Rose?" Sam asked. He looked annoyed.

Shivi realised she had crossed the line. However, to allay her uneasiness, Sam added, "This is for my mom. She appreciates sustainable clothing, and I'm sure she is going to love this."

Sam's reply was enough to wash away the embarrassment that Shivi had brought upon herself. After all, they had been good friends for quite some time now. A genuine friend always knows when and what to ignore. Sam had always been good at calming things down, whatever the situation.

Dhaani keenly observed Shivi's body language. She noticed that Shivi consciously stepped back. The girls also got dupattas for themselves. Meanwhile, Vivaan was busy satisfying his taste buds with delicacies like Kachri ki sabzi and Ker sangri at a food joint nearby. The trio joined him in tasting the food, and later, they began their return journey.

Noticing the behavioural changes in Shivi, Dhaani felt things had normalised by the end of the trip. Drawing reasonable inferences, she dropped the idea of talking to Shivi about the issue. She thought, *It is too early to express my doubts to Shivi. I should wait before I ask her anything regarding her expectations of Sam. She needs time. It might just complicate things for her at this point if I pose questions.*

Judging someone is easy

Because it is merely a one-sided conclusion.

But it's important to question one's judgement

And wait, for value gets attached to it

Only after relevant fact inclusion.

Chapter 7

More Trouble Brews at the Office

Back at the office on Monday, Shivi got the news of her promotion to the post of team leader. It turned out to be a classic case of confusion amidst jubilation because, with this promotion, she also had to shift to the office in East Delhi. Although a promotion is supposed to feel good, in some settings, it can send chills down the spine, courtesy of the atmosphere of scepticism all around.

Her parents were unaware of the awkward situation at her office, so when she informed them, they felt elated. She was also getting a raise in her salary, which was the need of the hour, as Sargam was going to join her in a year, and any amount of savings meant an enormous help to her.

Shivi moved to the new office and adjusted well within a week. However, this move also meant that the friends were going to meet less often. Dhaani and Vivaan, being busy with their study schedules, could not meet Shivi in person very often, but Sam always made it a point to meet Shivi on the weekends.

One afternoon, Shivi texted Sam and told him that she wanted to talk to him urgently. Sam came out of the office building and sat on a bench on the lawn. He dialled her number. She picked up the call immediately and said,

"Sammy, things seem fishy here. Remember, I told you a few days ago that a new cabin was being prepared? Our team was wondering who was going to join. You won't believe what's happening! Today, I got to know that Ranjan is now my immediate boss, and he'll be at this branch from now on. I just got an official email."

"What are you saying? How come no one came to know about it? He was here until yesterday. I was wondering why he hasn't come to the office today despite knowing about an important meeting that was scheduled for today."

"I don't know anything, Sammy. I'm just feeling so uncomfortable."

"Shivi, just relax. Don't worry. Just keep doing your job. You already have enough experience in dealing with him. He knows that I have your back. He won't dare to mess with you. I have to go to the meeting now. I'll catch up with you later."

Earlier, Shivi knew Sam would take care of any nuisance coming from Ranjan's side, but this move meant that she'd have to handle it all by herself. She felt a sense of unease but conditioned herself day by day to be on guard and began managing things better. However, trouble was undoubtedly brewing. Ranjan began pressurising her to go on day-long field trips with him every week. He coerced her into accompanying him to deserted relief shelters on the outskirts of the city twice. Consequently, she made it a point to ensure that she had a female companion with her at such locations. If there were other team members accompanying them for the distribution drives in slum areas, she felt comfortable. Whenever she got to know that she was going to be the only one accompanying Ranjan, for example, to a meeting, she made it a point to excuse herself. She even exhausted her sick leave for such reasons and had to show up at the office even when she was unwell.

When he couldn't have his way with her, he ensured that Shivi's interaction increased with him at the office. He changed her cubicle and got her shifted to the one which faced his cabin directly. She had no control over these actions of his. He assigned her work at the last moment and instructed her to complete it urgently. Often, this meant that she had to stay back at the office until late in the evening. Sam made it a point to go to the East Delhi branch and waited outside the office on such occasions. It started taking a toll on Shivi's mental state.

Ranjan crossed his limits with her on numerous occasions. He blamed her for mistakes that weren't hers and belittled her ideas. Being subjected to ridicule at the office was becoming a regular affair. The men in Ranjan's team even made immoral advances towards her a couple of times. Her only vent was the regular call to Sam while returning home from the office. She often broke down on the phone while talking to him. On one such call, when she was inconsolable, he reinforced her strength and said, "You are a strong woman. I don't think you need anyone's help to tackle that man or his assistants."

"I feel trapped, and I can't refuse the task he assigns," replied Shivi.

"Learn to have your way. This is how you will grow. Hold on to your integrity. Be fearless and fierce. He will have to back off. If he doesn't, then be courageous enough to report it to the administration."

Sam had seen many instances of female employees giving up or leaving their jobs at their office. It was déjà vu for him. After that call, he was in deep thought. *I can't let Shivi lose this job. Seems like she'll have to make a formal complaint because she is being nailed to the wall for fending off Ranjan's perversions. If she doesn't complain, it'll be just another win for Ranjan. He can't have it easy this time. One way or another, I have to help Shivi out.*

In the following days, Sam continued convincing Shivi to hold her nerve. However, things kept getting messier in the East Delhi branch. She was being mistreated by juniors in Ranjan's team. When she confronted or resisted, he often vented his anger on her in an outward rebuke for unthinkable mistakes.

One fine morning, Shivi resolved to hand in her resignation. She rang Sam up while travelling to the office. When Sam picked up the call, he was unusually happy— so happy that he totally missed the sadness in Shivi's voice. Even before she could speak further, he said, "Shivi, I was just going to call you. I have some great news."

Without waiting a moment, Shivi asked, "What's the news? Is it about Rose?"

"No, Shivi. I received a letter of appreciation today— for my performance—splendid performance, it said!"

"That's brilliant."

"Remember, I had told you about this philanthropist whom I had met at a distribution drive where one of our team members had got into a spat with a drunk man? This gentleman, who was passing by that stretch, had stopped his car to check what the issue was. He observed everything and later appreciated how I handled the situation. It got him interested in knowing Seva Troop's area of work."

"Yes, I remember you also went to his office for a presentation."

"Exactly! Appreciating our team's trait of going beyond our duty to help the needy, he has donated an enormous sum to Seva Troop for philanthropic causes. He watched us and mentioned in his letter to the management that my leadership was unmatched during the night-time drives."

"Really? Was he watching your work?"

"Yes, his team was keeping an eye on us to ensure that the money goes into the right organisation."

"Finally, at least someone realised how dedicatedly we do our job!"

"Yes, absolutely. The management is happy about this donation. They've arranged a special meeting this Friday at the office at 4:00 p.m. You must take a half-day off and come for it."

Sam's success story took over, and Shivi's resignation idea lost steam. She dropped the idea that day. Upon reaching the office, Shivi informed Ranjan that she was going to take a half-day off on Friday.

Ranjan said, "There is a lot of work in the office. You can't go to this employee recognition meeting."

"I will finish the work and then go. I wish to attend the meeting. Our entire group is going to be there. Also, I have leave pending for this month, and I'm just requesting you to approve it."

He departed without answering. She wasn't surprised at his attitude. The day arrived, and Shivi's leave hadn't been approved. However, she defiantly attended the meeting.

Sam's mother, Mrs. Fernandes, also came for the event, and Rose accompanied her. However, it wasn't a surprise for Shivi, as Sam had shared earlier that they were coming to the event. He introduced Shivi to his mother extremely warmly. After greeting and hugging, Sam's mother introduced Rose to Shivi. She said, "Meet Rose. She is Sam's friend."

Shivi greeted Rose and said to Mrs. Fernandes, "Yes, Aunty. We've met earlier." The fact that Mrs. Fernandes referred to Rose as Sam's friend was enough of an assurance for Shivi. It soothed her emotions.

That evening, Shivi's concern had inexplicably shifted from Ranjan's misdemeanour to Sam's joy and then to Rose's presence. Throughout, she noted that Mrs. Fernandes talked equally to her and Rose, not displaying any special affection for Rose. When Sam brought his appreciation certificate, he just hugged and kissed his mother. Other than that, there was no special out-of-the-ordinary display of affection towards Rose. That evening itself, Shivi got the impression that Sam and Rose were just being friends, and she found herself at peace. She was aware Rose was indeed a prospective bride for Sam; however, she didn't get carried away. Sometimes, emotions defy the facts, and maybe exactly that was happening now. A lingering, unexplained happiness was there in her demeanour in the days that followed.

A couple of days later, there was a face-off between her and Ranjan at the office. This day, Seva Troop's internal committee for women's welfare was to visit the office in East Delhi for a routine briefing. While the arrangements were being made in the conference hall, Ranjan mistreated Shivi and, to her advantage, one of the senior members of the committee, who had arrived early, witnessed it. She became concerned, and after the briefing, she separately called Shivi for a meeting at her office.

She said to Shivi, "As a practice, we purposely take measures to uncover unacceptable behaviour and unfair practices in the organisational structure. My early arrival was one such step. I noticed that Mr. Ranjan held your wrist and thrust the file into your hand. This action got me concerned because this is indeed unacceptable behaviour. Does this happen regularly here, or was it out of anger? Why didn't you report it?"

It was a silver lining in the clouds for Shivi. Shivi fearlessly recounted the mistreatment dished out to her on various occasions. The lady noted all the details. Shivi told her about events that had happened at the office in Connaught Place, too. Since Sam also had some information to share, he was also called by this lady to her office. Subsequently, the committee ordered a covert investigation. The committee also sent a two-member team to the flyover spot in order to dig deeper into the allegations levelled against Ranjan by Shivi and Sam. Luckily, this time, a lady from the clan recognised Ranjan's picture. She was the widow of one of Sam's attackers. But she didn't testify formally. So, the committee for women's welfare now had the details but no proof. The committee also asked Sam and Shivi to bring proof against Ranjan.

One day, Sam confronted Ranjan and purposely used a hidden camera to record the conversation. He questioned Ranjan, "What is the matter, man? Why are you imposing restrictions on Shivi?"

"What restrictions are you talking about? It is none of your business. Don't you dare interfere in my work!"

"Your work! Oh yes, I'm well aware of your work and your work ethic. You'd better not mess with Shivi."

"Look here, Shivi is my subordinate. I will treat her the way she needs to be treated."

"Forget it. I think you only understand when the management talks you down."

"Do whatever you can, Sam Fernandes!"

While saying this, Ranjan left the table. Sam's effort to record something concrete had gone in vain. Things between Ranjan and Sam took a grave turn at that very moment.

A week later, Sam got a termination notice. He wasn't surprised at all because he knew Ranjan was hell-bent on getting him out of his way. He thought, *Ranjan has crossed all limits. It is a do-or-die situation. I'll ensure that he faces the music this time.* Sam gave a formal written complaint to the management, seeking time for a meeting. He asserted that if he didn't get a satisfactory reply, he'd have to file a police complaint, as he suspected Ranjan's misdoings behind this move. Unlike before, he wasn't ready to ignore the management's bias towards Ranjan.

A meeting was scheduled, and Sam was called to the head office to explain his grievance. There, he presented several pieces of evidence, which he had gathered in anticipation. Other than Shivi's and his own experience, he presented CCTV footage of a couple of female employees who had exited Ranjan's cabin in a distressed, teary-eyed state. He explained that Ranjan was throwing him under the bus for reasons totally unrelated to his work at Seva Troop.

The investigating officer countered, "This does not prove Ranjan to be wrong. He might have just rebuked them over something they might have done wrong."

"Sir, I knew you were going to doubt it, so I even talked to these former employees. I got to know that one of them had resigned a week after this incident and shifted to another city. Then, I connected with the second one, who is now working at an NGO. She said that she could say nothing because he has connections with troublemakers, and I must leave her alone. She was not ready to testify. I couldn't convince her to help me. Just because I cannot prove it does not mean the matter doesn't need further investigation."

"So, there isn't any concrete basis on which we can ask Ranjan anything. Please try to understand that we can't ask him questions directly, at least at present. He has connections."

"But you can at least watch his activities. He threatens me, and I have a recording of his. If the company does not take action, I'll have to go to the police and let the law take its course."

After a heated discussion, they assured him that they would keep a close watch on Ranjan's activities. They assured Sam that his termination from the company would be reversed and marked the date for a follow-up meeting.

Interestingly, one day, Sam received an anonymous call, and the caller told him that he knew Sam was looking for proof against Ranjan. He offered to share some information. Sam became curious and cautious. He couldn't rule out the possibility of a plot to frame him and declined the offer. A week later, the caller contacted him again. Sam warned him that he would report his call to the police if he called again.

A day later, late at night, the doorbell rang. Sam got up and noticed that it was 10:00 p.m. He asked who was at the door. A desperate man replied, "I need to talk to you, Mr. Fernandes. I'm Sunil, an ex-employee of Dairy Good Food. You came to our facility in Gujarat some time back. Please open the door. I need to talk to you."

Sam opened the door and was surprised to see this man, covered from head to toe in a rough, grey blanket.

He looked to be in shambles. His hair was unkempt, and his face was smothered with black colour. Sam was apprehensive about letting him in, but then the man pleaded, "Sir, please let me in. My movement is being monitored. I beg of you."

Sam allowed him and then shut the door. Once inside, the man removed the blanket and wiped the grease off his face with his handkerchief. He began talking. He said, "I was there at the branch when you had come for an inspection at Dairy Good Food. I'm sure you haven't forgotten that consignment!"

"The mismatched consignment! Of course, I remember. Your company had then fired the culprit who was guilty of misconduct."

"I'm the one who was fired, and a case was also filed against me."

Sam got up from his chair and was about to reach for the vase on the table in self-defence when the man raised both his hands and said, "Don't worry. I'm not here to harm you. Believe me, Mr Fernandes."

"Move towards the door, or else I'll throw this vase at you," Sam said in a defensive tone.

The person moved as directed and then said, "I'm here to tell you it was Ranjan's plot. I called you twice in the weeks gone by. I asked for money, but only because I need it direly. My wife has left me. I don't have money to pay the lawyers. I lost my job. Ranjan hatched the plot, and since the time I asked him for my share of money, he hasn't been responding to my calls. He had promised to help me if things went haywire. But he backed out! I need help. Please, Mr. Fernandes. Believe me."

"But why are you telling all of this to me now? The matter is already closed."

"The matter may be closed for everyone, but not for me. Ranjan had promised me a huge sum of money in the first place, and that tempted me. He promised me a job in Delhi in his company. Then he went back on his promise. He even got me threatened to stay silent."

Sunil teared up and almost choked while speaking. He added after a pause, "Where do I go? I need your help. I'm ready to testify against him. After all, I also need some money to survive. When I met you in Gujarat, I judged your character. You are my last hope."

Sam dropped his guard and told Sunil to relax. They then had a long and detailed discussion.

Sam thought, *the investigating committee had proof against Ranjan for financial irregularities that were pointed out in the last audit. Sunil's statement could be the last nail in the coffin. Ranjan would be ousted immediately. I must write an email to the investigating head and inform him about this development.*

He emailed the details and, luckily, got an appointment for 11:00 a.m. the next day. Sunil slept at Sam's place that night because they were to head straight to the office the next morning.

The next morning, when Sam reached the office with Sunil, he was in for a surprise. He dropped Sunil at the entrance and went to park his car. At the parking lot, he saw Ranjan's sedan, which he didn't expect at all. He rushed from the parking lot to the entrance to inform Sunil. However, by the time he reached, the tables had turned. Sunil had vanished, and this left Sam flustered. Consequently, he had to face tremendous embarrassment, as he could not produce Sunil in front of the investigating team.

When the water gets murky,

It's wise to hold on to safety;

There can be a trap at every step.

To pull one in readily.

Chapter 8

Camping and Some News

A couple of weeks later, all four friends planned a picnic on the weekend because Dhaani and Vivaan needed to unwind, and all of them hadn't gone out together in a long time. Sam told them he had picked the Dabchik tourist resort as their destination this time. He excitedly explained, "It's a serene place in Hodal, Haryana, and is approximately ninety kilometres from Delhi. We'll be going in my car. You all will love the outing."

Vivaan immediately said, "I'm going to drive half the distance, Sam."

Sam agreed readily, as he knew Vivaan enjoyed sharing the driving duty with him on their road trips. Dhaani and Shivi were excited and began discussing what they'd be wearing for the trip. However, amidst the chit-chat, office work popped up. One of Ranjan's aides rang Shivi and told her, "Ranjan sir has scheduled an urgent meeting at 8:00 p.m. in the office today."

"Today? Are you kidding me? I left the office barely two hours ago. I'm not coming again," Shivi retorted.

"A request had come in from an NGO for a food distribution drive on the outskirts of the city where a convoy of pilgrims travelling to Chandigarh is holed up. You have to lead one of the three teams. That's the only information I have, and Ranjan sir has ordered that you have to be there."

"Let him pass whatever order he wants. We can't be working according to his whims and fancies."

"I suggest you talk directly to him."

"Listen—you can tell him that I won't be coming."

She refused point-blank and put down the phone. A couple of minutes later, Ranjan called her. He reprimanded her and said, "How dare you defy my order? Don't forget that I'm your boss. You are going to lead one of the relief teams tonight, and that's final. Be there on time or else be ready to look for another job."

"Sir, with due respect, I would like to inform you that your demand is against the company's policy of assigning only male staff for emergency night shifts. Correct me if I'm wrong. The only thing I can do is coordinate remotely."

"To hell with the company's policy! I think you need a taste of all that I can do."

Shivi kept her calm and said, "You need to calm down. I know my rights as an employee of Seva Troop. I'm not your slave. I will escalate this matter to the committee for women's welfare. I am being fully cooperative and offering to coordinate the work remotely on compassionate grounds. Despite my best efforts, you are threatening me with repercussions!"

Ranjan realised that this could land him in trouble. He angrily ended the call and later assigned her duties to another team member. Shivi had become firm and bold in handling such matters after shifting to the East Delhi branch. Sam, Vivaan, and Dhaani, who had listened to the conversation, reinforced her strength and applauded her approach.

The next day was a bright one. It was sunny and lightly breezy. While they were en route to Dabchik, Sam got a call from Rose. Vivaan mischievously picked up the call, pretending to be Sam. He turned on the speakerphone. Sam struggled to snatch his phone back but couldn't, so he intervened and began talking while everyone heard the conversation. Rose asked angrily, "Where are you, Sam? I've been trying your landline number for the last hour!"

"Rose, I'm travelling. I'm with my friends. We're going on a day trip."

"You didn't even ask me! How mean of you, Sam!"

"It was a sudden plan, Rose. We decided yesterday evening. Even if I had asked you, it wouldn't have been possible for you to join us. Please get real."

A brief argument ensued. The situation was awkward for Dhaani, Vivaan, and Shivi. Vivaan turned off the speaker to spare Sam from any further embarrassment. It became evident that she wasn't happy at all, and her authoritative traits were also unexpectedly revealed. Even after a few more minutes of convincing from Sam, she remained unsatisfied and abruptly cut Sam off. Dhaani was stunned and felt sorry for Sam. Reaching out for Dhaani's hand, Shivi expressed her astonishment. Stupefied, Vivaan made eye contact with Dhaani through the rear-view mirror. She stared in disbelief. There was a lot of unease, and none of them spoke a word for a good five minutes! Sam murmured something, though.

To get off the topic, Vivaan asked Shivi, "How's it going, Shivi? Since Ranjan moved to the branch in East Delhi, we've not had much information about him, though yesterday's incident amply told us you continue to be between a rock and a hard place."

Before Shivi could say anything, Sam jumped into the conversation and said, "That scoundrel! He's stooped to new lows!"

Vivaan thought, *Bingo, Sam! This question was for you only—not Shivi!*

Vivaan's trick to change the topic had worked. Sam responded very well to Vivaan's intelligent move. His discomposure was obvious. Perhaps Rose's misbehaviour had made him a bit nervous. It looked as if this attempt from Vivaan to change the topic was what Sam was also waiting for.

Vivaan spontaneously asked, "What happened, Sam? Did he mess with you too?"

"Yes, he stealthily tricked me!"

Surprised, Vivaan began listening keenly.

Sam added, "Recently, a man approached me dramatically and told me he was ready to testify against Ranjan in the case related to Dairy Good Food. When I took him to the investigator's office to record his statement, he disappeared from the gate itself."

"Oh, my God! I can't believe it," said Vivaan. He added after a pause, "Sam, tell us more about it."

The girls also listened keenly. Sam then explained all that had happened. On listening to all of it, Shivi said, "Sam, there can be two possibilities. One being, the man wasn't lying. It is highly likely that spotting him at the office, Ranjan would have made him disappear. He's capable of doing that. You mentioned Sunil said that he was being watched!"

"That's also possible, but we can't rule out that Ranjan may have planted Sunil. However, the bottom line is that Ranjan got away once again! I should have been more cautious. He has always been clever enough to stay in the good books of the top authorities. It is so difficult to prove him guilty of misconduct. The management also brushed under the carpet the grey areas highlighted in the yearly audit report. That wasn't a minor issue either, but in the end, his team was cleared after levying a mere penalty."

The discussion continued. After some time, they reached the resort and headed straight for lunch. It was now time to leave behind all workplace issues, as enjoyment was now their sole aim. After a sumptuous lunch, they stepped out to enjoy the fresh air, the breathtaking landscaping, and the quacks of ducks. The greenery turned out to be the perfect soother for each of them, and their togetherness energised them enough for the regular daily grind.

After the enjoyable outing, while they were returning, Sam again got a call from Rose. Initially, he avoided picking up the call. However, he eventually answered it at

Vivaan's insistence. It was a brief call, and Rose apologised for her misbehaviour. She told him she had lost her temper earlier because she had to face the hassle of him not answering the landline.

Soon, Sam himself began talking about Rose with his friends. He somehow wanted to share his deepest feelings. After all, he needed someone to hear him out since his close friend, Shivi, had never been receptive to him talking about Rose. Today, he had the company of Vivaan and Dhaani, who offered him much-needed and unprejudiced attention.

Sam elaborated, "Sometimes, I find it so difficult to understand Rose. She has an unpredictable temper. The last time I went to Nagpur, I wanted to meet her. My mother was also eager to see her, so we invited her over for lunch. She happily accepted the invitation. We prepared a special lunch for her, and she backed out at the last moment, saying some guests had arrived at her place. My mother was disappointed at her cold and irresponsible behaviour. Then, that same evening, she told me to extend my trip by a day because she wanted to go for dinner at an upscale restaurant with me. However, I declined as I had to come back to Delhi because of prior work commitments. I don't like it when she acts childish. There are some days when she wants to know everything about my plans. At other times, she doesn't even take my calls. Her moodiness irritates me, but I continue to have a soft spot for her. I appreciate her candour, although she dilly-dallies sometimes."

Sam was opening up forthrightly, yet gently.

Vivaan playfully remarked, "Sam, you're not a special creature on this earth. It's the same with all girls. Isn't it, Dhaani—my darling?"

Dhaani frowned upon hearing this. She gave him a stank face and said, "I hate you, Vivaan!"

This drew belly laughs from all. Their trip ended with Sam dropping off Dhaani and Shivi at their homes. Vivaan stayed the night at Sam's place, and their day concluded on a lively note.

Six months zoomed past, and one day, Sam got an early morning phone call from Rose. He was busy tying his necktie and still had to set his hair before leaving for work. There was a slight quiver in her voice—a quiver of excitement. She said, "I have something to say, but I don't know if this is the right time. I'm getting butterflies in my stomach."

"What's the matter, Rose? Come on, tell me. I don't think our conversations were ever that formal," he continued to complete the Windsor knot.

"Yes, I agree. So, I'll just say it in one go. Don't stop me or react in between," said Rose.

"Okay, I won't. But you're making me anxious."

"Ah ... so, looks like I have developed some new feelings."

"What feelings?" he picked up the hairspray while speaking.

"I told you not to interrupt. I'm nervous."

"Rose, is this about us—about you and me?"

"Yes ... yes ... yes! I think I'm falling in love with you."

"Oh, my God!" Sam put the hairspray on the dressing table and pulled out his study chair. He sat and added, "Are you serious? I mean—you aren't joking, right?"

"So funny! Why would I be joking, Sam?"

"Rose, I'm so happy to hear this. Even I was praying secretly for this. Have you told your parents about it already?"

"No, I had to tell you first!"

Sam's eye crinkles, jolly tone, and happy tears testified to his patient and eager wait for this moment. Out of excitement, he fluffed his hair and messed up the well-set hairstyle! He felt silly at that moment.

He said, "Okay. Then let me surprise my mother with this news first."

"Let's surprise her together. You plan and come to Nagpur for the weekend."

"That's a brilliant idea, Rose."

He chalked out the details of his visit and conveyed them to Rose. They decided to reveal the news a little dramatically to Sam's mother because she had been wanting to hear this for a long time.

The next evening, while he was out with his friends enjoying ice cream, Sam revealed the news. Unable to contain his excitement, he said to Shivi, "I have some good news to share."

"I could guess there's something going on. Your smile is different today," Shivi said as her eyes shone with excitement.

Dhaani giggled along with Shivi and said, "You're right, Shivi. What is it, Sam? Are you getting a raise or a promotion?"

Vivaan intervened and remarked, "Girls, I bet it's not related to work! His face looks lit up today."

"Guys, let me speak!" exclaimed Sam. Nervously rubbing his left hand on the back of his head, he added, "You're right, Vivaan. It's not about work at all. It's about Rose. She said *yes*."

"Superb!" exclaimed Vivaan and gave Sam a tight hug.

Dhaani added teasingly, "Wow, Sam. Lucky you!"

Shivi accidentally dropped her vanilla-flavoured softy cone on the floor. However, she was quick to ignore it. She said, "Congratulations, Sam. You never even hinted at anything before. I thought she had friend-zoned you!"

"Yes, Shivi. Even I had no clue. She rang me up yesterday and told me about it."

"Great, so when is the wedding?" asked Shivi, although with a bit of indifference.

"Well, we still haven't conveyed the message to our families. We plan to meet and break the news together to my mother first."

A fun banter began between the boys as Vivaan began teasing Sam. An hour later, Shivi told Dhaani that she was tired and wanted to go back home. It was clear in her body language—not that she was faking uneasiness or something. This time around, on receiving news about Rose, she was definitely more conscious of her conduct. Perhaps she had learnt her lessons, and Sam's and Rose's relationship status didn't affect her anymore. Perhaps she realised that Rose's entry into Sam's life would not endanger her friendship.

There was a lot of work to be done in the upcoming months at the office. Sam was handling the projects at the Connaught Place branch. Vivaan and Dhaani were busy juggling between their work and study schedules. The group met less often in those couple of months, but there wasn't any loss of contact. Dhaani kept a check on Shivi, assessing her attitude and well-being from time to time. Shivi was doing fine. However, she was up to her ears in chores. Along with focusing on work, she had to look for an apartment to rent because her sister, Sargam, was to join her soon.

At the office, it seemed Ranjan finally understood that Sam was not someone who would stay silent. Sam had cautioned him enough against mistreating Shivi. Ranjan's actions showed he had taken the warnings seriously. For how long this dangerously complicated equation between Ranjan, Sam, and Shivi would remain balanced was a hard question to answer. After all, the ego can step in anytime and ruin one's thinking abilities, especially so when the person is of considerable disrepute.

Life progresses, emotions change,

And thoughts change;

As far as intentions are clear and righteous,

There's nothing insane.

Chapter 9

Sargam's Arrival

Six more months had passed, winter was receding, and Shivi had been exceptionally busy setting up the new house that she had taken on rent. It had been just a week since she had shifted. Although small, setting up the one-room-kitchen apartment along with her daily office routine turned out to be a hectic affair. She asked Sam if he could help her. He happily assisted her with the shifting and related chores. For a couple of days, he routinely picked her up from the office and accompanied her to the market so that he could help her buy new furniture.

Shivi used to tell Sargam about the progress each day so that she remained excited. One evening, when they were on a call, Sargam enquired, "I'm watching a show these days. It comes at night on the Moon network, channel number six. Does that channel come on your TV in Delhi? I can't afford to miss it. If not, please get a subscription for that."

"I don't have a television here, Sargam! However, I have a laptop on which I watch movies. You can also watch with me once you are here. I'll get you some movie CDs on rent."

This information left Sargam flabbergasted. She screamed, "What? You haven't arranged for a TV set! I thought you'd even have a cable connection by now, unlike us here in the village."

Her mother had come running to her room after hearing Sargam speak so loudly. She asked Sargam, "What happened?"

Sargam desolately handed over the receiver to her mother and told her, "I'm not going to the city! Shivi hasn't bought a TV set. What kind of a better life am I looking at?"

Sargam's mother frowned as she took the receiver from her. Shivi was still saying something over the phone to convince Sargam. Her mother interrupted her and said, "Relax, Shivi. I'll handle this. Let me talk to her first."

She ended the call and began calming Sargam down. Sargam yelled relentlessly, just as a two-year-old would throw tantrums for a toy! All efforts from her mother went in vain, and the responsibility to convince her now lay with her father.

As expected, he too could not convince her. How could a father not melt seeing his daughter's tears? Subsequently, Shivi was told to buy a TV set. Her parents offered to pay for the television, as they knew she had already overspent in setting up the new abode. However, she declined their offer and assured them that Sargam's demand would be met.

The next day, both Sam and Shivi went looking for a second-hand TV set, and luckily, they got a good deal. The television connection was done in a jiffy. Shivi fulfilled Sargam's wish and informed her. It was only after this call that Sargam resumed her packing for Delhi. The doting elder sister also fulfilled a couple of similar demands, like one for a radio set and a bicycle! With dedicated efforts from both Shivi and Sam, the abode was finally ready within a week to welcome Sargam.

Finally, the moment arrived. On a fine, breezy morning in February, amidst the receding chill, Shivi waited at the railway station to receive Sargam. Sitting on a cast-iron bench, Shivi was sipping tea from a tiny earthen cup when she heard the announcement that the train had arrived. She gulped the tea and got up hurriedly to go towards the platform on which the train was arriving. The train was yet to stop, and Sargam waved at Shivi from her window. Shivi instinctively directed her to pull her hand back in. The excitement of stepping into the world of a metropolitan city for the first time in her life was distinctly visible. After a few minutes, Sargam exited the train, and Shivi hired a porter to help them with her bags—two large pink suitcases and two small ones. Within an hour, they were at home.

Sargam had been chatting all the time during the journey, about the city, the houses, and the parks that she was seeing. Once they reached home, Shivi asked the cab driver to help them with the bags, and he transported the bags upstairs for some extra money. When they were climbing the stairs, Sargam began talking again. Shivi said to her, "Please lower your voice a little. I know you're excited, but the residents here are old people, and you have to be soft. We can't be disturbing them."

"Am I too loud?"

"No, darling. Not too loud. It's just that we're blessed with a high-pitched voice, and I've learnt to lower it down living here in the city. Inside the house, things are different, but when we're outside or conversing with someone, we have to be soft."

"Oh, maybe it is the echo because of congested spaces. The village has so much open space!"

Shivi smirked at this logic of hers.

Sargam rested the first day, and then, the very next day, she said to Shivi, "I want to go for a sightseeing trip around the city."

Shivi said, "Sargam, you have just arrived here. It's a bit too early to take a trip around the city." She wanted her sister to settle down first, so she convincingly added, "I have already completed all the formalities for your school admission. The academic session begins in April. You have plenty of time; I'll take you out for sightseeing before you join the new school, I promise. But you must allow me some time too."

Sargam acceded to her request. However, her incessant pleas for an outing resurfaced merely twenty-four hours from then. Eventually, Shivi gave in and planned Sargam's first outing. It was a visit to the school that she was to join. It was a short outing because Shivi had time constraints and could manage only that much. Just after they were back, Sargam rang up her mother and began describing her day. She said, "Mummy, I'm so excited to tell you this. We both went to see the school today. Since it was a weekend, we just went around the premises. It's a magnanimous, multi-storeyed building with a vast playground. I spotted basketball hoops and badminton nets there."

"That's great. Now you can indulge in sports along with your studies. I'm glad that you're liking it there."

"Yes, and then Shivi took me to eat pani-puri and papdi chaat at a stall in the market near our home. It was yummy."

"That's lovely. But be careful to eat outside only once in a while. Don't fall sick before joining school. You must eat freshly cooked, nutritious food."

"Yes, Mummy."

Their talk lasted a few more minutes. Later, the sisters slept.

A couple of weeks after her arrival in the city, Sargam began feeling homesick. She was not eating properly. Bouts of crying punctuated Sargam's phone calls with her mother. Her parents were also missing her, but they didn't want to lower her morale further, so they pretended to be happy and busy with their regular chores. However, they guided Shivi to keep Sargam occupied and requested her to be lenient regarding demands for short outings. Through detailed calls with Shivi, they also kept a tab on Sargam's day-to-day progress as she began adjusting to the new environment. Shivi got their point.

A week later, when Shivi noticed Sargam hadn't slept properly for three consecutive nights, she became concerned. She thought of planning an outing for Sargam and requested Sam to help her out. Sam excitedly planned the outing as he always used to. He told Shivi, "As our priority is a teenager this time, I've decided that we'll take her to a cinema hall and watch a nice movie. Afterwards, we'll go to a new eating joint at Janpath to try out Chinese food. I've heard that this joint is bustling with customers, all thanks to affordable and tasty dishes on their menu!"

"That's a great idea. She'll be so excited to walk through the lanes on Janpath. I'll get her some nice dainty jewellery and some tops to go with her favourite pair of jeans."

As planned, they went for the outing and accomplished all that they had in their minds. The evening ended with all of them relishing different flavours of ice cream at a famous ice cream parlour.

Dhaani and Vivaan got Sargam a video game as a welcome gift to keep her occupied in her free time. Sam got her a mini radio so that she could listen to some songs and not get bored while Shivi would be off to work during the day.

In a month's time from then, she joined school. Studies gave her the required level of engagement and social exposure as she could interact with kids of her own age. Initially, she hit a hurdle there when she found it difficult to get friendly with her peers. However, it required little conscious effort from her, as she was brilliant in studies and that led to her being befriended by her classmates for notes, answer sheets, assignments, and all related help that she provided happily.

Once she was comfortable at school, she began interacting with the kids in her colony. Slowly and gradually, Sargam opened up. She even looked forward to those once-in-a-while outings with her sister's colleagues. These were the people who regularly pampered her with small yet interesting gifts. Sam began taking care of her as if she were his own little sibling. She, in turn, rewardingly used to say that he was her best friend!

Sargam's first year in Delhi went by swiftly, and now she was in the twelfth standard at school. Studies were getting tough owing to new subjects, higher complexity, and increasing competition. Therefore, Shivi got her enrolled in tuition classes for extra help and personal attention.

One day, Shivi returned home early. She wasn't feeling well and had taken a half-day off. Sargam was out for her tuition classes. Shivi was having tea on the balcony when she spotted Sargam with a group of boys on the street. When Sargam returned home, Shivi opened the door for her. Sargam was almost dumbfounded because she didn't expect her sister to be home so early. However, Shivi didn't directly ask her anything pertaining to the boys. Sargam settled at home, and while giving her a glass of banana shake, Shivi casually asked, "What about your friend Pooja, who used to accompany you to the tuition classes? How is she doing? I haven't seen her for a long time."

Sargam replied, "Even I haven't!"

"But she was in your batch? Wasn't she?"

"Yes, her mother got her batch changed last week."

"Okay, and what about Nisha? She used to accompany you back home. I haven't seen her either."

"Yes, she left the classes and joined another centre."

"Why? Has she shifted to some other place?"

"I don't know," said Sargam inattentively. Suddenly, the landline phone rang, and Sargam sprang up from her chair to pick up the call.

Shivi found this strange. She thought, *Sargam always refuses when I tell her to pick up the phone or get me a glass of water. Today, she is behaving unusually. Was she awaiting someone's call?* However, Shivi soon got busy preparing dinner and forgot about it.

The next Saturday, Shivi attended the parent-teacher meeting at Sargam's school. This was another big shock for her as all the teachers told her the same story of Sargam's failing attention and dropping grades. Shivi felt quite embarrassed.

The sisters hired an auto rickshaw for their trip back home. While on their way, she asked Sargam, "You study till late at night in the living room and are always in a hurry not to miss your tuition. Then why is your performance dropping?"

"The teacher at school just dictates notes and then leaves. She doesn't explain things properly."

"Then most of the children should complain, but that isn't the case. You go for tuition, too. Isn't the tutor able to help you out?"

"No, the tutor is great. He clarifies all concepts."

"Then why is your performance poor?"

"We haven't started studying these chapters in the tuition yet."

Shivi continued to question Sargam for a while. However, Sargam could not give satisfactory answers to most of Shivi's queries. Subsequently, Shivi subtly warned Sargam of dire consequences if her performance didn't improve. Perhaps that was all she could do at that moment.

After about two months, the four friends planned another sojourn. Sargam was in her village for a week, so Shivi could accompany her friends. They set out with fervour and energy on their journey to the foothills of the Himalayas for a two-day residential camp. Meeting after a considerable span of time, all four of them were equally excited to spend the next couple of days in each other's company.

It was an eight-hour drive, and they hired a cab because Sam wasn't interested in driving such a long distance this time around. He seemed tired and somewhat dull, too. Comfortably seated in the back seat of the seven-seater, the girls binged on chips and muffins and talked their hearts out. Vivaan and Sam had their headphones on and slept during most of the road trip.

At the resort, both Dhaani and Shivi headed to their room while the men thought of venturing out, as they had already slept during the travel.

During the outing, Vivaan casually asked Sam, "So, when are you planning to get married?"

"What plans? No plans!"

"Why so? Rose is too busy, it seems!"

"The chapter of Rose is closed."

"What? How come?"

"It's a long story and not so pleasant. I'll tell you about it some other time."

Sam sounded melancholic, so Vivaan refrained from probing any further. Maybe this was the reason Sam had opted for a relaxation camp this time.

When Sam and Vivaan returned to the resort, the girls were up after their nap. So, all of them had coffee and some nice cottage cheese sandwiches. Then they attended a lecture on meditation. It was a great session focused on maintaining emotional harmony amidst the external chaos. They were given an introduction to meditation techniques and explained the importance of mindfulness. Afterwards, they went for dinner, which was specially curated by in-house Ayurvedic experts. It had tasty and nutritious dishes, keeping in mind the recommended diet. After dinner, they all wished to watch a movie, but they were too tired to go out to a movie theatre. Subsequently, they began watching one on the laptop. Halfway through the movie, Sam dozed off. Even Shivi didn't find the film interesting enough, so she excused herself and went to her room. Vivaan seized the opportunity to tell Dhaani about Rose. He began talking to Dhaani. He candidly asked, "Did you notice any change in Sam?"

"Oh yes, I did. He sounded very low. I thought of asking him, but didn't find time to do so."

"I asked him."

"What did he say?"

"He's upset because of Rose."

"Why so?"

"They broke up."

"What are you saying? That's so sad!"

"Yes, it is. However, he didn't tell me much. He seemed so disheartened."

"I'm sure it would have been from her side. He seemed thrilled with this alliance."

"Even I think so."

"Although I haven't known her closely, I can say that she had a pretty fickle mindset."

"I agree, Dhaani. Remember, Sam told us how she always changed her plans at the last moment?"

"Yes, and he also said that she had a bit of a hot temper."

"But this is bad news. Now I understand why Sam was so desperate for this trip. We must help him overcome this phase."

"Yes, absolutely," Vivaan looked at the wall clock and added, "Dhaani, it's already half past midnight. I think you should go to your room now. Shivi had said she won't lock the room and would wait for you."

"Yes, I must go. You take care of yourself and Sam, too. I'll see you in the morning."

"Good night, dear."

The next morning, after the meditative session, Sam seemed better. Sitting at the breakfast table with his friends, he said that he wanted to talk about something to all of them. He then broke the news that Rose had shifted base to a foreign country a month ago. Shivi was stunned. She looked towards Dhaani, who nodded. Sam teared up, and Vivaan comforted him by holding him close. Dhaani whispered to Shivi, "Vivaan told me about this last night only."

Shivi asked Sam, "But Sammy, how did this happen?" After a pause, she added, "I mean, were you not aware that she planned to go abroad?"

Sam was heartbroken and replied in a sombre tone, "She mentioned nothing! I feel cheated. She got married to another guy and shifted without even letting us know."

Shivi asked, "Wait, what? She got married! How can that be? What about her family? They were in Nagpur only. How come they kept such a big move under wraps?"

"They managed it very well. They didn't take my mother's phone calls for a week after Rose had stopped taking mine. At first, I thought she might be upset over something. You know how she was—she used to go silent whenever stressed or angry! So, I thought I'd go to Nagpur to find out because I was clueless. Then Mom said she'd try to find out first. So, she tried calling Rose's mother's phone, but there was no response. After about three days, she went to their place and found their house locked. Their neighbours told her that the family had gone for an outing last week and hadn't returned since. Then I dialled her office. I could connect with her boss, who told me she had got married three days ago and was now in London. She had resigned two weeks ago."

None of them could say a word after hearing all of this. They had always seen his joyous side. This was the first time they were seeing Sam in such a disheartened state. He needed the warmth of friendship to cut through the chilling pain of heartbreak. Perhaps it was more than heartbreak—it was a void from being deceived.

The retreat turned out to be therapeutic, but the effect lasted for only a week. Subsequently, he became quiet and reclusive once again. His liveliness took a back seat. On some days, he seemed to work like a machine, but never did the degree of his kindness towards the needy reduce. Even on the gloomiest of days, he made it a point to visit some or other relief shelter. This was above and beyond his ambit of duties, and he took along hot food for the needy. He sat with them, listened to their struggles, and found solace in spending time with them. It was his way of lightening—his way of getting the burden of thoughts off his chest.

His friends knew well that this was what could bring light back into his life. They helped him, offering all the emotional support that they could. His mother also came to Delhi and stayed with him for a week during this time.

Life peculiarly reveals its intricacy

At an opportune time.

While it may not be the most suited moment

According to us,

On the larger screen, things eventually fall in line.

Chapter 10

In the Grind

One day, at the Janmashtami celebration in the colony, Shivi met a few ladies whom she had consulted before getting Sargam enrolled in the tuition classes. A general chit-chat turned into a shock for Shivi when one lady said, "Why is Sargam still going to AMN Tuition Centre? I have pulled out both my kids. In fact, most of us here have got our girls enrolled in other coaching centres."

Shivi became concerned and asked, "I didn't know about this development. May I ask you the reason behind this move?"

The ladies standing there seemed worried. They began discussing the issue with Shivi.

A lady said, "Shivi, how can you be so careless? Didn't Sargam tell you anything?"

"No, I don't have any clue about what you all are saying. She just said that two of her peers had left the tuition when I enquired."

"Shivi, the boys enrolled there were misbehaving in the classes, and the tutor wasn't doing enough to control them. The tutor didn't bother to finish the syllabus on time and kept the students involved in casual and unnecessary activities. He even cancelled the tests twice, and instead, they all watched movies on his laptop with him."

The ladies said that they even warned the tutor, but he didn't mend his ways. All of this shook Shivi to the core.

Shivi was angry when she returned home and wanted to talk to Sargam about it. However, she got a call from Sam, who was already on his way to her place, along with Dhaani and Vivaan. He had planned to go for a short drive around South Delhi to see the decorations and celebrations at a couple of temples. She decided not to create a scene as it was a festival that day, and any discussion would have spoiled everyone's mood.

The next day, while dropping her off at home from the office, Sam asked Shivi, "Shivi, you didn't seem so pleasant yesterday. Is everything alright? You seemed lost while we were at the temple. I saw you were on the brink of crying."

"Sargam is in the wrong company. I'm totally shaken. How could she do this?" Shivi broke down as she said this.

"What happened? What did she do?"

Shivi gave an account of the discussion she had with the ladies in the colony the previous evening. Sam was visibly upset too. He said, "Shivi, you must get Sargam enrolled at another tuition centre ASAP. It is your responsibility. You both are away from home, and you have to take care of her."

"Yes, I understand that. It's so difficult to handle this girl. She answers back all the time. This city has changed her completely. She was a disciplined child when she was in the village."

"Shivi, it often happens when there's such a tremendous change. And it's just unfortunate that Sargam fell into that trap of throwing teenage tantrums."

"I feel that I should have been more aware of what was going on in her daily life."

"Shivi, you can't be blaming yourself entirely for it. You are at work for eight to ten hours. And think about it this way—it's not too late. There's still time for her final exams. It's all going to be alright. Calm down and be firm with Sargam."

At home, what resulted was a series of intense discussions, as Sargam was reluctant to accept that she was at fault. Shivi had the habit of keeping things to herself and didn't bother her parents with any of her issues. However, this time, when Shivi couldn't handle Sargam's rebellious nature, she finally rang up her mother and told her about it.

Next, Sargam received a brief call from her mother. She plainly said to Sargam, "Shivi has told me everything. I'm disappointed. If I get another complaint from Shivi, you'll be called back here. Even your father would not help you out then. Shivi is providing you with a safe foundation to build a good future. If you continue like this, we'll withdraw these privileges."

Her mother didn't say a word extra and ended the call, expressing her anger. This call worked like magic. The warning was just enough, and Sargam agreed to change her tuition teacher.

Shivi got her enrolled in another tuition centre, and it was an all-girls batch this time. She formulated a rather firm set of instructions, and Sargam had to abide by them. Shivi sat her down one evening and said, "Sargam, now that you have started your new tuition classes, I want you to pay attention to your studies. I am going to be in constant touch with your teacher from now on to get updates about your performance. Don't mess around this time."

"I get it. Can I go to my room now?"

"No, I'm not done yet. From now on, I shouldn't see you hanging around with the boys in the colony."

"I never hang around. We play basketball!"

"Sargam, I know what I'm saying, and I don't want any arguments. Get this straight. You will get to play in the park for an hour in the evening. From today onwards, you won't be going to any of your friends' homes to play."

It was a harsh step. Shivi didn't have a choice but to go into damage control. Sargam had no choice but to follow the instructions.

Three months later, Sargam's grades hadn't improved much. However, she had become more disciplined. Shivi believed that she was on the right track, so she continued with the strict routine. At one point, the only distraction left in their home was the television. Soon, Shivi had to sever the TV connection as well. Finally, after her constant efforts, numerous checks on Sargam's performance, and conscious conditioning, the child improved and later passed her twelfth class with distinction.

Passing high school was just an initial yet essential part of the journey that Sargam had embarked upon. The next two months were even more crucial, as she had to appear for entrance examinations for institutes of higher education. Shivi wanted her to be admitted to a technical course and guided her on that. Sargam also had to give interviews for a couple of colleges.

The rapport between the sisters improved considerably after Sargam completed high school. Shivi allowed her more time to interact with friends freely. Sargam was undoubtedly enjoying the culmination of the schooling phase because she was now again getting the independence that she had wished for. Shivi was having a tough time loosening controls, but she knew she had to do it because she wanted a smooth transition from school life to college life for her little sister. Sargam was still the rebellious kid somewhere. She began demanding more and more. She wanted to go out for movie nights and wanted to be in the company of friends most of the time. She always countered Shivi's strictness by saying that she wasn't a school-going child anymore.

Day in and day out, they had such arguments. Shivi could not manage it and didn't want to disturb the parents, too. So, she talked to Sam about it and asked him for help, as Sargam listened to him.

Sam stepped in, as he thought Sargam needed to be guided on the right track. He visited them one evening and took them for a drive around the city. Sargam loved to be driven around, behaving like the little child who would throw tantrums to sit in the front seat of the car. She even used to ensure that only songs of her choice played in the car.

While driving, Sam began talking to Sargam about how she had achieved a major milestone by completing her high school. He delicately implied to her the importance of safety in today's harsh world.

He told Sargam, "Shivi is so brave and intelligent. The way she has managed everything is commendable."

"Yes, I know, but she has your support, too. Everyone looks for support from friends. You must tell her to be open-minded. She never lets me have any male friends. She is up in arms whenever she sees me with boys."

Shivi was about to intervene when Sam said, "Sargam, you are misunderstanding your sister. She talked to me about that issue and told me that the boys you were befriending were not worth your company."

"But how does she know about that? I wasn't going around with them. They were just my study mates."

"Darling, they need to be just study mates. Shivi rightly sensed that they could take advantage of you. Moreover, she came to know that there was no up-to-the-mark study going on at the centre. I'm sure you can't deny that. Your academic performance was dropping. Wasn't it?"

"No, I'm not denying it. That chapter is already closed. I went to a different tuition teacher at that time."

"Listen, dear. Your sister is just trying to help you because she wants you to avoid making the same mistakes she, or anyone she knows, has made. She is concerned about your safety because she has taken up your responsibility. I don't know if Shivi ever told you about her own struggles.

When she first came to the city, I was her mentor at the office, and I had to save her from so many nasty people at the office. Many a time, even the clients can mean trouble in the workplace."

"No, she never told me or Mummy about it."

"It's because she could not trouble the parents with these issues. Do you know we give self-defence training to female staff as soon as they join the office? The stage at which you are is even delicate. If an endangering situation arises, you won't be able to fend anyone off. It's imperative that you get the hang of things first—before you explore life the way you want to. Young brats can cause even more trouble. You all are at a stage where immaturity can make you vulnerable. Don't you want to get settled well? It's just three more years of dedicated study, and you can set your career rolling. We come across so many kids in campus interviews who take the wrong track, score very low, and remain unemployed. We look at their grades and also their all-round development. You must join college and then take up some personality development activities. This is the time to channel your energies if you wish to lay the foundation for a bright future. You have your whole life to enjoy."

Shivi saw Sam could guide Sargam, and Sargam also listened patiently. She wasn't challenging Sam's ideas anymore.

When they returned home, Sargam was polite with Shivi too, way better than before. She talked to Shivi respectfully and said, "I understand that you would have faced many issues when you came to the city. Thank you for guiding me."

"Darling, I can totally understand your emotions. I'm so glad that you now understand my perspective."

"Sam is so intelligent. He made me understand things the right way. He was so polite. You have always been so strict with me."

"Oh, my God! You feel that way about me! That's mean," Shivi smiled and pretended to be annoyed.

"No, I'm not being mean. That's the reality. He's a genuine gentleman and a perfectionist. He has superb taste when selecting food outlets, movies, and books."

"Sargam, I think we've had enough of a discussion about Sam. You seem impressed by Sam, but know that he is my friend first. Treat him like an elder brother, not like a friend. You ought to treat him with respect and reverence," Shivi said in a dominating tone.

Sargam frowned and went to her room. Shivi was also tired. They both slept early that night.

Subsequently, Sargam got serious about studies and gave it her best. In the days that followed, Shivi was greatly relieved as Sargam finished her entrance examinations and finally got admission to a Bachelor of Mass Communication Course. Although Shivi wanted her to join a technical course, she was satisfied with what Sargam had accomplished, considering how her performance had been in the past year.

Responsibilities at different stages in life

Reveal certain intricacies

That make us think deeply,

And timely notify us of dangerous fallacies.

Chapter 11

A Snake in the Grass

Sam and Shivi had successfully revived their deep and warm connection after a gap period of almost a year. Sargam had a sizeable role to play in it, as it was her presence and the trailing complexities which had brought Sam and Shivi even closer. During these last couple of years, both had experienced some intensely emotional moments. For Sam, it was Rose's exit that had made him reset his priorities, and Shivi stuck by him through it. For Shivi, it was Sargam's entry that brought conflict and confusion. Both Sam and Shivi felt as if they were actually raising a teenager. Sam always attended to Sargam as if he were her guardian. Shivi saw a new side of him as he guided her with issues related to Sargam. Consequently, she felt immensely grateful and their bond deepened.

After Sargam had joined college, Shivi's responsibilities and duties had become lighter. She now had some time to spare. There was no need to prepare lunch for them because Sargam usually returned late in the evening, and Shivi managed from the office canteen. Now, they also had a washing machine at home, and Sargam helped Shivi with household cleaning on weekends. Sargam had developed an interest in drama, so she joined a theatre class with her peers at college. By the time Shivi returned home, Sargam was already there, and she sometimes pampered her sister by keeping tea and store-bought snacks ready for her elder sister.

Shivi could concentrate more on her work now. She was looking for a higher role in Seva Troop. Sam also began meeting Shivi frequently, either at her place or at a cafe.

Shivi felt satisfied that Sargam's schooling was over, and so were her parents. During one of her regular calls to Shivi, her mother casually enquired, "So, how was your day?"

"A day at the office is always hectic, Mom. But it's more relaxed at home now since Sargam manages most of her stuff herself."

"Does she study, or is she busy with her friends most of the time? Whenever I call her, she's out somewhere and says that the college class got cancelled."

"Oh, Mummy! It happens in colleges all the time. I'm sure she's saying that to you even when they are on a mass-bunk! I try to ignore these things. As long as she keeps the right company and it doesn't become a routine affair, I don't mind."

"Yes, I know the kids in metropolitan cities are very outgoing. We also don't mind giving her that much liberty."

"How's Daddy doing?"

"He is fine. Presently, he's out to get some milk from our neighbour, as we ran out of it today."

Then the bell rang. Her mother put the call on hold, as Shivi's father had returned home. Shivi talked to her father as well and then retired to bed.

One evening, when Sam came to drop Shivi off at her place, Sargam invited him over for tea. Honouring her invitation, Sam stopped by. Sargam surprised him with an elaborate high-tea menu. She had enrolled in cooking classes recently, and the child in her wanted to showcase her talent. However, there were certain little details that pointed towards another track—impressing Sam for unknown reasons.

Sitting in her chair, Shivi pointed to the bouquet placed on the side table and asked Sargam, "Who got these flowers?"

"I bought them. Their deep colour seems to ooze love. Aren't these red roses beautiful?"

"Of course, they are beautiful. But when did you develop a liking for flowers? When I tell you to water the rose plant on the balcony, you never bother to listen. You never helped Mom with gardening either."

"Don't you think you're being rude, Shivi?"

The conversation was going to spiral into an argument, so Sam intervened and said, "Oh, Sargam! Your sister is just pulling your leg. Isn't it, Shivi?"

Shivi understood Sam's intention and smiled to maintain the peace at home.

While relishing the feast, Sam said, "Sargam, you've put your heart into preparing this spread. All the dishes are so delicious."

Sargam replied, "Thank you so much."

Shivi said, "All of this is genuinely good, but a little spicy for me."

"She's made it for me, Shivi. She knows my taste!" said Sam teasingly.

Sam was great at handling dicey situations.

Shivi never approved of Sargam's subtle yet overly sweet gestures towards Sam. She always seized the opportunity to school Sargam rightly regarding her behaviour towards males. Knowing that Sam was too mature to take it otherwise, she expressed it all openly. It was mutual trust between them that kept insecurities at bay. A fun banter ensued, and then Sargam went to the kitchen to fetch some more tea.

While they waited, Sam told Shivi, "Vivaan and Dhaani have failed in their attempt at the civil services exam. The results were declared this afternoon."

"Oh my God! They must be very upset. Let me call Dhaani," said Shivi and picked up her phone to call Dhaani.

Sam stopped her and said, "No, you must wait for things to settle down a bit. Vivaan is with her. I talked to him, and he told me that Dhaani wanted to give up on it now. He doesn't want her to quit. He wants us to convince her to get back to studies and take the exam again the next time."

"That is going to be a hard task. She was already so done with the hectic study pattern. She told me a few months back that she was just going to try one last time. It really takes a toll on one's emotional health. I was so sure that they'd crack it this time."

"Even I was of the same view, but some things aren't in one's control at all."

Then Sargam came back, and they began talking about her college again. Later, Sam left, and the sisters went to sleep.

Subsequently, Shivi planned to meet Dhaani to talk to her about this aspect. She booked a table for two at a nice, newly opened cafe. She took Dhaani along on the pretext of trying out the food there. It was a cosy eatery on the terrace of a three-storey building in the market's heart. The ambience was amazing, and there were golden fairy lights all around. The girls made themselves comfortable in the velvet-cushioned armchairs and began talking. Shivi said to Dhaani, "I think I chose the wrong place!"

"Why? What happened? It seems pretty good to me."

"Look around—all lovebirds here! And the music being played is also romantic!"

"Oh yes, I didn't realise that. The ambience has captivated me since the moment I entered. Agreed—all love birds out here. Look at the ones on the table next to the railing—how cutely they are holding hands—totally smitten by each other!"

"Dhaani, stop looking that way unless you want that man to outstare you!"

"Let's order some food then, so we can get busy laying our eyes on the dishes," Dhaani winked at Shivi and grinned.

As they waited for the food to be served, Shivi began talking as per her plan. She asked Dhaani about her civil services exam results. Dhaani tried to brush the discussion aside, but Shivi persisted and advised Dhaani that she wasn't doing the right thing by quitting at such a crucial stage. She said, "Dhaani, you've already studied so much. It's just some more effort that's required."

"I know, but I just don't have any mental strength left to give it another try."

Just then, a couple entered the terrace and walked up to the table next to them. The man, dressed in all-black attire, courteously pulled out a chair and made his lady sit comfortably. He gave her a peck on her hand before he sat. They looked mature, and Dhaani couldn't help but stare at them, too.

Shivi hit Dhaani's foot pretty hard under the table and tried to regain her attention. Dhaani grimaced in pain. The next moment, she said, "Look at them. They complement each other so well. Such a beautiful couple! I picture myself and Vivaan like this a decade from now. His height matches Vivaan's exactly!"

"Oh yes, you're right. Indeed, they look so good together. Some couples have this magical aura about them."

"I'm surely bringing Vivaan here next time. This place has a charming vibe," said Dhaani, as she tilted her head to one side and ran her fingers through her hair dreamily.

"Yes, bring him for sure. In fact, when are you both settling down? Any plans soon?"

"No such plan, Shivi. He hasn't even proposed to me formally as of now!"

"Oh, come on, Dhaani. Is there any need for all of that? I mean, you know your own mind. You both complete each other. He's so caring and you share professional aspirations, too. Yours is a perfect match—a match made in heaven."

Dhaani began blushing and then asked, "What about you? Is there anyone on your horizon?"

"Dhaani, you'll be the first person to know if someone enters my life!"

"Of course, I know that. Actually, I wish you find your soulmate soon. You've been so dedicated to your family and now to Sargam. I want you to experience these beautiful feelings before your hair turns grey and your face gets wrinkled!"

"What? Wrinkles and grey hair? Do you see any already?"

Dhaani laughed her heart out and held Shivi's hands warmly. Then she said, "No, my darling, I was just being naughty. But yes, I feel it's high time you find a partner. Are your parents looking for a groom for you?"

"No, they've left it to me. They are the most understanding people in my life. I'm blessed to be their daughter. I wish my special someone is as protective and loving as them."

"Wow, so some expectations are already there!" exclaimed Dhaani.

The conversation continued. The girls thoroughly enjoyed the evening, relishing great food and talking their hearts out. Shivi blushed a lot when she opened up and began talking about her hopes for a partner, and Dhaani noticed it. After the awkward episode related to Rose, Shivi had never talked about these things. It was now that Dhaani gave her a comfortable and cosy space to open up.

The next evening, Vivaan called Shivi to enquire about Dhaani's reaction to her convincing and counselling. Shivi kept beating around the bush because she had failed at her attempt to convince Dhaani. She thought, *What have I done? How do I tell Vivaan that we talked about everything under the sun except the civil services examination? It's my fault. Had I selected another place, we wouldn't have got distracted, and I could have convinced her to give the exam another attempt. What will I say when Sam asks me about the same?*

Vivaan was pretty irked by her confused reactions. She brushed off his questions by saying that she would talk again to Dhaani. Shivi was in a fix, more so because she had recognised her own feelings about settling down in a relationship when she opened up to Dhaani the previous evening. Up to now, Shivi and Dhaani hadn't ever talked about marriage and settling in such detail.

Dhaani, who was unaware of Shivi's hidden intent, spilled the beans when she talked to Vivaan the next day. Vivaan immediately understood why Shivi couldn't give him a satisfactory reply the day before. He was in splits on realising Shivi's position. He thought smilingly, *Shivi is such an actor. Her tone conveyed nothing of this sort! She pulled it off so well. However, it's great that she poured her heart out to Dhaani at least. She needed to acknowledge her feelings and the desire for a life partner. Away from home, taking care of her younger sister, she practically has no one to share these things with. I'm sure she'll prioritise talking to Dhaani about the exam the next time she talks to her.*

A week later, one day, Sargam went to visit her sister, Shivi, at her office unannounced. On seeing her, Shivi exclaimed, "How come you are here, Sargam? You should have called and informed me."

"I came with my friends. We had lunch at a cafe nearby. Ruchika had her birthday today, so she gave us a treat. I thought of surprising you. But it seems you aren't happy to see me."

"No, Sargam. That's not the case. I just meant that it would have been better if you had informed me beforehand."

"I have a meeting in ten minutes from now. You can stay here in my cabin until I return. Let me get you a coffee. As it's Friday today, Sam will be here in another two hours. Then we'll go back."

"Don't worry, I'll stay here only. I have to do some physics file work. I'll finish that."

In the evening, Sam arrived to drive them home. While on their way, Sam stopped at an ice cream parlour because he knew Sargam loved ice cream. That night, when Shivi was preparing dinner at home, she got a phone call from one of Sargam's friends. The girl on the line enquired if Sargam was fine. Surprised, Shivi asked her, "Sargam is absolutely fine. Couldn't you reach her?"

"I tried her number, but found her phone switched off. I just wanted to know about her well-being."

"She is fine. You people just met a few hours back. Then why are you so concerned? Wait ... did any of you fall sick after the lunch party that you people had today?"

"What party are you talking about? Sargam had said that she was unwell, and she left for home before the lunch break. I just returned from college and thought of calling her."

"What? Didn't you go out to celebrate Ruchika's birthday today?"

"No, Ruchika's birthday was last month. We didn't go out anywhere today. We were at the college, and Sargam left after half a day, saying that she was sick."

They hung up. Shivi was confused. She knew that something was not right, and knowing Sargam's nature, she decided not to ask her directly. Instead, she wanted to find out the truth for herself. However, she knew Sargam would be ready with a cover-up story as soon as her friend conveyed the details of her talk with Shivi to her. So, she immediately talked to Sam about it, who took a neutral view and said, "You shouldn't have asked her friend about the party directly. You could have kept the details to yourself. Maybe it was some other group with whom Sargam went out. She might just be hiding it from this girl. It happens very often among youngsters."

"But this girl is her bestie. They go shopping together. I don't understand why Sargam lied to me. I have to find out why she came all the way to the office."

Sam said, "Shivi, keep your inquisitiveness under control. Keep a check on her activities. Just stay silent this time because if you talk to her right away, she'll give some excuse and brush it off. Try calling Sargam often or keep in touch during the day with text messages."

Shivi said, "Okay, then I'll just tell her to keep me in the loop if she goes out of the college premises. I'll say that it's for her safety and security."

"Shivi, I know you are hot under the collar, but you'll have to handle things patiently. If she turns hostile, she'll become even more vulnerable and may pick up some vices out there. If you say anything of this sort, she'll obviously ask the reason for such restrictions!"

Shivi got so stressed that she had tears in her eyes. She said, "It feels like I'm raising a kid of my own. This is so difficult and scary. I want to protect her, but she won't understand it."

Sam comforted her and calmed her down. He convinced her not to say anything to Sargam and instead tighten her vigil.

A month later, Sargam again landed at Shivi's office. This time around, she came with her friends and brought one of them along to meet Shivi at the office. No new doubts cropped up, but the mystery behind Sargam's prior visit remained unsolved! Shivi was liberal enough to brush it off as teenage behaviour and ignored the incident.

However, she was unaware that there were clouds on the horizon.

Soon, Sargam began frequenting Shivi's workplace. Sometimes she said that she came shopping at a book market nearby; sometimes it was for lunch with friends, and sometimes it was for group studies at a friend's place, who coincidentally lived near Shivi's office. Interestingly, ninety-five percent of her visits were on Fridays. Shivi was disturbed by this routine because Friday was the day Sam usually came to pick her up from the office and drop her off at home. Both used to look forward to this hour-long drive to share updates from the week gone by. However, with Sargam accompanying them, they hardly had time to talk.

One afternoon, Ranjan noticed Sargam's presence and asked Shivi to introduce her. Ranjan, a habitual flirt, knew very well how to approach young girls. Sargam wasn't an exception, and he began talking to her. He made her comfortable in Shivi's absence. In a casual interaction that lasted less than five minutes, he extracted crucial information from her, like the details of her college, her course, college timing, etc. Shivi had to take a phone call, so she had gone out of her cabin briefly. Even before Shivi returned, they had exchanged phone numbers.

Sam arrived in the evening. While in the car, Sargam talked to Shivi about her interaction with Ranjan. Shivi asked her, "Why did you give your phone number to Ranjan?"

"I didn't give him the number. After you went out to take a call, he began talking to me. Suddenly, I realised my phone wasn't in my pocket. I began searching for it in my bag. He helped me by making a call from his phone so that my phone could be located."

"Oh, Sargam. You are too naïve to understand men like Ranjan! It was just his way of getting your phone number. He is a shady character. Get this straight—you need to stay away from him."

"You always find faults in anyone I talk to—especially if it's a male."

"No, Sargam. You're taking this discussion in the wrong direction. I know him way better than you do."

"No, you are being unreasonable."

"I can prove my point right away! I know him very well."

"Then prove it."

"Okay, tell me where your phone was."

"It was beneath him. He accidentally sat on my phone."

"Exactly. He hid it first so he could get your phone number. From the time I've been working here, I've heard about such incidents an umpteen number of times. Now, just follow what I say. Stay away from him."

Sargam said nothing and instead began searching her handbag for something. Her ignorance angered Shivi. Sam, who had stayed silent during the heated conversation between the sisters, tried to gesture to Shivi to calm down while he continued to drive.

Then Shivi asked Sargam, "Why do you always wear so much makeup when you come to my office? You don't wear it every day to college, do you?"

"What's wrong with you? I mostly come after outings. I'm dressed and groomed accordingly."

"But today you came this side for group studies, so why this dramatic eyeliner, bold lip colour, and showy danglers? What's the need?"

Sargam blatantly ignored Shivi. She surely didn't see eye to eye with Shivi on the issue. Sam noticed in the rear-view mirror that Sargam was sneering and looking at him as if he'd support her in mocking Shivi. He adjusted the mirror to avoid eye contact with Sargam because he knew Shivi was right and supported her. He dropped them home, and the day ended.

A week later, one evening, when Shivi returned home, she could smell the smoke of cigarettes. She asked Sargam, who said that the whiff might be from outside. When Shivi went to the bathroom, there was a strong and overpowering sandalwood fragrance. Shivi came out instantly and asked Sargam, "Why did you spray so much perfume in the washroom? I couldn't even breathe."

"The washroom was smelly, so I sprayed the room freshener. It's not perfume. We don't even have sandalwood perfume, do we?"

"Sargam, I don't want this discussion. I've had a long day at the office, and I'm tired."

"What's the big deal? Turn on the exhaust fan if you find it so uncomfortable."

Shivi went back. After washing her face, she reached out for the face towel, and it fell. While picking it up, she noticed some ash on the floor. She understood Sargam was up to something. Later that night, she secretly checked Sargam's bag. She found a pack of cigarettes, a toothbrush, and toothpaste in there. She took the cigarette packet out and threw it away.

The next morning, Shivi confronted Sargam regarding the cigarettes. She said, "I found a pack of cigarettes in your bag yesterday. I threw it away, but I'm going to inform Mummy about it today."

Sargam was shocked and said, "It is my friend who smokes, not me! She had put it in my bag because she didn't want to take it home. At least you should have asked me before throwing it away."

"Do not play these games with me. There was ash on the bathroom floor. Now, you'll say that your friend came and smoked cigarettes in our washroom!"

"What ash? I don't know what you're talking about."

While saying this, Sargam began walking towards her room. Shivi was angry. She pulled Sargam back by her arm and said, "Listen to me, I haven't finished yet."

Sargam forcefully removed her hand, and a verbal spat ensued between them. Sargam began shouting and verbally abusing Shivi. Unable to tolerate such grave misbehaviour, Shivi slapped Sargam. Sargam was red with anger. She picked up her bag and left for her college without saying another word. Subsequently, Shivi also left for her office. The whole day, she felt guilty about being harsh on her sister. She talked to Sam about it during lunchtime. He told her that whatever the situation was, hitting Sargam was wrong. To calm things down, they planned to pick her up from college. Both took a half-day off. Luckily, Ranjan was also on leave, so Shivi could excuse herself from the office easily. Had he been there, he would have refused to grant leave to her, citing some reason or the other. Shivi and Sam left for Sargam's college.

During the drive, Sam kept explaining to her that she should be patient with Sargam, considering her tender age. Shivi accepted that she had made a mistake and agreed that she needed to control her aggression. When they were nearing the college, Shivi called Sargam, but she did not pick up the call. Shivi tried again, but there was no answer. She became anxious. However, much to their relief, they spotted Sargam at the college gate. They proceeded to take a U-turn in order to reach the gate. Shivi was eagerly watching Sargam, and when they were barely fifty metres away from the college gate, a car approached Sargam. She sat in the front seat, and the car drove off. Astonished, Sam sped up and began following the car. Shivi made many calls to Sargam, who didn't answer and later switched off her phone. Shivi was perspiring due to stress, and tears were rolling down her cheeks. Anger had made her hands and feet tremble. Sam began driving faster, being careful not to miss the car in which Sargam was sitting. He told Shivi, "Don't worry, I'm catching up. We'll get them at the next stop signal."

"I didn't expect this from her. She shouldn't have avoided my calls! This girl has crossed all limits."

"We're almost behind them. See, that sedan is just about a hundred metres ahead of us." He pointed towards the car and then added in a suspicious tone, "Why do I feel I have seen this car earlier?"

Meanwhile, Shivi started chanting a mantra, her hand tightly clutching a picture of her spiritual guru. Sam was getting closer to the sedan with every passing second. Somehow, he was keen on checking the number plate of that car. The vehicle ahead of them indicated a right turn, and Sam accelerated. As soon as he pulled up to the sedan, the traffic light turned yellow, and the sedan zoomed ahead while they had to stop. Shivi exclaimed in despair, "Oh no! They're gone!"

Sam immediately said, "Dial Ranjan's number and give the phone to me."

"Why should I dial his number? What are you saying?"

"Shivi, do what I'm saying. This car was Ranjan's!"

"What?" While saying this, Shivi almost choked.

"Yes, I had a doubt since we began chasing them. I confirmed it from the number plate."

Shivi burst into tears and dialled Ranjan's number, but unfortunately, his phone was on voicemail, so she had to end the call.

Sages have said that teenage is a tender phase.

You never know what thoughts prevail

Until you befriend a child of that age.

Because if not done correctly,

Nothing can be of avail.

Chapter 12

Friends Come to Their Rescue

Despite Sam's strong assertion that Sargam had boarded Ranjan's car, she blatantly denied it. She said it was her friend's car and her phone was in silent mode. Shivi was in distress after the incident and wished to call her mother over to Delhi. However, Sam assured her he'd handle things, as he knew Sargam would listen to him. He explained to her that bothering the parents was not a wise thing to do, as it would add to their woes, and they'd get stressed unnecessarily. He was of the view that if she had taken up the responsibility of her younger sister, she ought to handle it patiently. To comfort her, he explained that with Sargam's safe return, any potential harm had been avoided. He explained to her that some youngsters do get swayed and display such behaviour. The environment of metropolitan cities is such that young adults feel free. Shivi also understood that since she was away from her parents, Sargam had no one other than her or Sam who could teach her to align her choices with her goals for her future. The matter ended there.

Two weeks later, one evening, Sam stopped by Shivi's place to have a word with Sargam. He had previously directed Shivi to let him talk to Sargam in his own way, so Shivi stayed out of it by pretending to be on a phone call with a friend in her room. Sargam was happy to see Sam, as usual. She excitedly prepared frothy coffee for him and also some sandwiches to go with it.

Sam told Sargam, "You make excellent coffee."

"Thank you. How did you like the sandwiches?"

"Oh, they're tasty too."

"Once, I had similar sandwiches at Shivi's office and loved them, so I tried to replicate them. I'll pack some for you, so you won't have to make dinner tonight."

"You're being so nice to me. Even I love those. By the way, Shivi told me you're still connecting with Ranjan. She was concerned because she saw you talking to him in the office last week."

"Not really connecting! She exaggerates everything."

"Don't get me wrong. It's not that we're complaining about it, but I just thought that you needed to know how that man is. I've worked with him for a long time and have always told interns to be cautious around him. He is indeed cunning."

"Why do you say so? He seemed like a gentleman to me."

"That's exactly my point! He behaves in such a manner that you won't even come to know what is going on in his mind."

Sargam snubbed Sam and said, "I can't understand why you people think about him this way. He comes across as an urbane man."

At this point, Shivi, who was secretly listening to their conversation, felt that Sam's polite talk would not help to solve the matter. So, she came out into the living room and intervened, "Sargam, I had advised you to stay away from Ranjan. You have breached my trust. I can't be polite anymore. I'm warning you again to stay away from him."

Sam was visibly upset with Shivi. However, keeping a cool head, he requested her to stay out of it.

Meanwhile, Sargam protested. Banging her fist on the tabletop, she said to Sam, "Oh, now I get it! She has told you about her insecurities, and you are trying to brainwash me. I didn't expect this from you, Sam."

The coffee mugs rattled, and coffee was spilt on the table because of Sargam's aggressive action. Shivi shouted angrily, "Sargam, behave yourself! Sam is older than you."

Sam got up from his chair, took Shivi to a corner, and told her to stay silent. Then he calmed Sargam down and explained to her a few instances of how Ranjan had tried to mess with Shivi at the office. Sargam listened to all that he said and later, somehow agreed not to be in touch with Ranjan. Perhaps she had no other choice. Perhaps she didn't want to annoy Sam. Subsequently, Shivi got Sargam's mobile number changed so that Ranjan couldn't reach her.

Afterwards, Shivi warned Ranjan in strong words to stay away from Sargam. It was all she could do, as curbing his lecherous intent was not in anyone's hands. She exercised control over Sargam because that was within her power, up to an extent. For some time, she kept reminding her sister that she needed to stay away from Ranjan. Every now and then, she talked to Sargam about how he had always troubled her at the office. Perhaps Sargam genuinely listened. Perhaps she pretended to do so.

One day, Ranjan emailed Shivi a couple of pictures of a girl sitting at a restaurant. The girl's face wasn't visible, but her side profile matched Sargam's. She immediately enquired with her sister, who outrightly denied any recent interactions. Trusting her, Shivi thought it might be his tactic to create unrest between them and ignored it. Another time, Ranjan sent a picture of Sargam standing at the edge of a pavement on a road and wrote that Sargam might be in danger. She called Sargam, who said that she had just boarded a bus to return home. Shivi realised Ranjan was following Sargam. She thought of filing a police complaint against him. She discussed it with Sargam, who got anxious and requested Shivi not to do so, thinking it would involve her unnecessarily. With no option left, Shivi ignored this act of his.

Over the next two weeks, Shivi realised that Sargam had taken her advice lightly. Though initially, she had shown signs of anxiety, she ignored Shivi's concern and didn't bother to tell Shivi about her whereabouts when going out with friends.

When she talked to Sam about the emails, he said that there couldn't be better proof. In his view, Ranjan had finally faltered by sending her those pictures in emails. He advised her to complain to the management but cautioned her not to tell Sargam about it. Shivi realised it was the right thing to do. She lodged a mental harassment complaint and presented the evidence to the committee for women's welfare. On examining the evidence, they referred the matter to the management. Shivi requested a transfer back to the Connaught Place branch, citing safety reasons. Her request was accepted, and Ranjan was also warned of dire consequences by the Head of the committee for women's welfare at the company. Because of his influential contacts and closeness with the top management, the matter was closed after he gave a written apology to Shivi.

A month later, at the Connaught Place branch, things seemed settled for Shivi. She could work peacefully. Both she and Sam tried to keep a strict watch on Sargam. All four friends were together once again at the office, and joy began spreading its wings. With Sam and Shivi seeing each other every day, Vivaan somehow got the idea of playing cupid between them. He felt the need to take on his duties as a close friend.

Vivaan began prodding Sam openly now and then, deciphering his feelings for Shivi. He gave those cosy feelers to Sam in interesting ways. One day, while Sam was picking up some chocolates at a store, he saw Shivi's favourite candies, so he picked up a pack of those to surprise her. Vivaan asked Sam, "Why didn't you get any for Dhaani, and why not for me? I bet you don't even know Dhaani's choice."

Sam understood Vivaan was up to some mischief. He replied, "What are you trying to say? Of course, I know about Dhaani's choice." He nastily added after a pause, "I don't need to remember yours, though." They kept teasing each other and continued shopping.

On another day, when Sam brought homemade besan ladoos from Nagpur, he offered them to all in the office and kept a separate box for Shivi. Vivaan searched Sam's locker and laid his hands on that box and teasingly asked, "Why is so much favouritism going on? Am I missing something?"

"Stop it, Vivaan. You know how much Shivi craves these ladoos, so I got a separate box for her. That's it."

Somewhere, this constant nudging from Vivaan made Sam understand his feelings for Shivi. After some time, Vivaan told Dhaani that it was the right time to make Shivi aware of her feelings. Both Vivaan and Dhaani could see that their friends were a perfect match, but previous incidents had complicated the situation. Vivaan wanted Dhaani to take up the cause of making Shivi understand the likelihood of a great companionship between her and Sam. Although she agreed to talk to Shivi about it, she had some doubts about why and how to broach the topic with her. Understandably so, because she had seen a sea change in Shivi's behaviour when Rose had entered Sam's life. She asked Vivaan, "Are you confident that Shivi would agree with our line of thought? I mean, I can surely say that she had feelings for Sam earlier, but when Rose came into the picture, Shivi took a step back. Can we rightly expect her to rethink her decision, even if Sam thinks positively regarding a probable alliance?"

"Dhaani, you're being too critical; matters of the heart are way simpler!"

"No, I don't agree with that. We cannot force Shivi to mould her feelings according to the other person's availability. I get a feeling that it might be a closed chapter already. They are good friends. Honestly, I'm afraid to ask Shivi about it."

"But we never openly talked to her about it, Dhaani."

"Vivaan, we may not have asked her directly. But she's intelligent enough to know what we were thinking when we asked her indirect questions."

Seeing that Dhaani wasn't convinced, Vivaan said, "I get your point. Would it be better if Sam first decoded his feelings and then approached Shivi himself?"

"That would be much better, because, in that case, the matter would stay between both of them. It would be more comfortable for Shivi to express her liking if she has feelings for Sam."

They planned to continue giving gentle feelers to Sam about the same.

On various occasions, Vivaan subtly talked about Shivi's nature with Sam. He noticed that Sam appreciated and paid attention to every little detail. After a couple of months, when Vivaan was convinced, he finally sat him down and said, "Sam, you need to realise that you have feelings for Shivi. You aren't totally unaware of those. I mean, you enjoy each other's company. You gel so well. Then why are you hesitating to take the relationship route?"

Sam replied, "Shivi is undoubtedly a precious friend. I know we get along very well. In fact, after Rose's betrayal, I don't even think I'd be able to trust anyone easily for a marital alliance. The thing is that I cannot lose my friendship with Shivi at any cost."

"Why would you lose your friendship? Do you think Shivi is that immature?"

"Of course not, Vivaan. But in case she isn't of the same view as us, she might just distance herself from me if I talk to her about all this."

"Sam, you are not a stalker from whom she would distance herself. You are her friend, and when you express your feelings, you'll come across as frank and honest! Otherwise, you'll go on secretly admiring her like anyone else. I'm sure she wouldn't appreciate that at all."

After an hour-long discussion, they returned to their homes as the night was pitch dark, and Sam had enough to ponder over.

A week later, Sam planned an outing for all four of them on the outskirts of Delhi. They were to go to a handicraft fair. Vivaan backed out at the last moment and ensured that Dhaani also refused, as he wanted Sam and Shivi to go for a peaceful, private outing. He didn't do it in a hidden manner either; he talked to Sam a night earlier and told him, "I already had plans for tomorrow, but if I had told you, you wouldn't have planned this outing. Dhaani is also skipping this outing because we both want you to get serious and ask Shivi about what she feels. We're concerned for both of you. You never know, Shivi's parents might think of getting her married. Don't think that this friendship will last you a lifetime after you both get married to different partners. That only happens in fairy tales. If you both make such a great pair, why can't you just be together officially? And, of course, if Shivi doesn't share the same thoughts as ours, which I genuinely doubt, at least you won't have any regrets for not having tried."

Sam understood his point and thanked him for thinking about them. Now, he was also sure about talking to Shivi.

The next morning, Sam and Shivi set off in his car for the handicrafts fair. While on the way, Shivi felt nauseous, so Sam stopped the car along the roadside. He gave her some water, and once she felt better, they set off again. The fair was about ten kilometres from there. Shivi developed a headache, and Sam was concerned, so he stopped midway to get her some fresh lime juice. "I haven't had breakfast; that's why this is happening," said Shivi.

Sam became concerned and asked, "Why didn't you tell me earlier?"

He brought out a box from his bag and gave her a sandwich to eat, which he had brought along. She felt better after eating, and they carried on.

At the fair, the major attraction was a dance performance by folk artists. The enthralled visitors cheered the artists, and it was a lively affair. Shivi was so excited that she couldn't resist grooving to the performance. She grabbed Sam's arm and made him do little dance steps as the audience also began enjoying the performance in front of the stage. Amidst the festive vibes, Sam's eyes gleamed as he got the much-required confidence to reveal his feelings to Shivi. It seemed as if this was going to be the day when they would begin their journey as a couple. At least the aura indicated that.

Apart from the dance performance, there were huts where traditional crafts were being showcased. There were dip-dye stalls for the creative enthusiasts. Mehendi artists were busy decorating the hands and arms of ladies with organic henna. There were woodcraft stalls where home decor items were the hot sellers. In summary, the fair had a resplendent display of the country's heritage. The earthenware stall with live pottery making was the one that instantly attracted Shivi. She even tried creating an artefact at their do-it-yourself counter. Sam was happy to see her express happiness after a long time. He hadn't seen her enjoy this much in the last six months. Ranjan and Sargam had brought a lot of stress into her life.

After spending an hour enjoying the exhibits, they headed to a nearby food stall to have lunch. While eating, Sam thought of starting the topic.

Taking a deep breath, he said, "Shivi, I want to talk about something which might have some impact on the way we are today."

"Sammy, you're scaring me! What is it? Did I annoy you by pressuring you to dance with me?"

"No, not at all. In fact, I enjoyed that bit the most."

"Okay." Surprised, she asked, "What is it then?"

"Shivi, this is serious."

He paused for a moment and drank some water.

"Shivi, I have developed a liking for you."

"What? You didn't like me earlier? I'm shocked to hear this!"

"Shivi, get serious."

"Okay, Sammy. Go ahead, I'm listening."

"I believe I'm ready to take our friendship to the next level, if you feel likewise."

This day, Shivi's behaviour wasn't in tandem with her inherent intense and sensitive nature. She avoided answering completely and instead questioned, "What do you mean by the next level? Are you going to buy me some jewellery as a mark of our friendship?"

At this moment, Sam somehow lost confidence. Shivi's jocular remarks added to his dilemma. Ignoring Sam's discomfort, Shivi took the last bite of the ladoo on her plate. The way the talk was progressing didn't quite encourage him to go any further. Meanwhile, Shivi spotted a lady who was selling pickles, and she quickly pulled Sam along to walk towards the stall. They purchased a few from the wide range of savoury pickles and later began their return journey. However, Sam didn't let this failure affect the mood of the day. He came across as excited during the return trip as he was in the morning. Shivi also maintained her expressions. Perhaps she understood his intention but didn't want to anger or misguide him, either.

As soon as she returned home, she rang up Dhaani and requested her to come to her place. Dhaani knew that something had happened, so without asking questions, she left for Shivi's place.

As soon as she saw Dhaani, Shivi became emotional. Dhaani leapt towards her and hugged her tightly. Then she made her sit comfortably. Dhaani thought, *I was so right when I told Vivaan that Shivi would not accept Sam's offer. This poor girl! She'll have to go through all of it again.*

Shivi said to Dhaani, "I don't want to be the second choice."

"Second choice? What do you mean by second choice, Shivi?"

"Sam tried to propose to me today. I don't want to be his second choice."

Dhaani's viewpoint changed immediately. She thought, *I was wrong. Shivi isn't uninterested. She just needs to know that she holds so much importance in Sam's life. Vivaan might be absolutely right. God is great! We can help Sam and Shivi now.*

She calmly told Shivi to look up and asked her, "Did he? What did he say?"

"He was trying to talk about it. I knew where the conversation was heading, but I didn't want to answer that question. I just can't accept being the second choice!"

"It's not a case of being a second choice at all, Shivi."

"Of course it is. Have you forgotten Rose?"

"His mother had arranged that alliance. He wasn't involved romantically prior to that. Shivi, you have forgotten that he developed a liking for Rose over a considerable span of time. They became friends first, and then she agreed to marry him. If you look at it in the right way, you'll know that he just accepted her proposal."

"But the thing is that he also wanted to be with her. He accepted her and looked forward to her company. So, she made a place in his heart. Had she not backed out, he wouldn't have asked me at all. They would have been happily married. I already went through a lot when Rose entered his life."

"I know all of that!"

"No, you know nothing! Dhaani, you know absolutely nothing!"

"Darling, we've been friends for a long time now. Neither Vivaan nor I mentioned it to you, but we knew Rose made you quite uneasy for whatever reasons."

"That time, I didn't even know what was going on in my head. I was in an emotional mess. I felt I had lost my precious friendship in just one go. It has taken us two years to get back to normal. And now—today—this happened."

"Shivi, tell me one thing. Will any girl who comes into his life as a partner be his second choice?"

Shivi sobbed, then shook her head, and said in a low voice, "No."

"Why are you thinking that way, then?"

"Because I was there in front of his eyes when he chose Rose."

"Okay, but can you say that he chose Rose over you?"

There was a pause—a lull—a silent moment of realisation.

Dhaani asked her again, "Can you say that he chose Rose over you?"

Shivi nodded. Dhaani comforted her in an embrace and added, "Sam wasn't even aware of his feelings for you until last month!"

Shivi stared at Dhaani and wiped her own tears. Dhaani gave her some water to drink and then began explaining. She said, "Vivaan had to prod Sam to decipher his intentions and emotions. We saw what you both were not seeing. From our perspective, you both are perfect for each other."

Shivi was too stressed to understand anything beyond this. Dhaani realised she was overwhelmed, and it was tough for her to accept Sam's proposal at that moment. Sargam was out on a college field trip to Goa. So, Dhaani stayed with Shivi for the night. Dhaani told her, "Let's just have dinner. You need to get some rest. Sleep properly, and we'll talk about this tomorrow with a fresh mind."

The next morning, they woke up to a thundering sky and roaring clouds. Dhaani made coffee for both, and they sat comfortably on her tiny yet aesthetically decorated balcony. Shivi began setting the bougainvillea vines right so that she could see the flowers and feel the softness in her hands. Dhaani knew Shivi was introspecting, and they spent their coffee session in a cloud of silence. Then, Shivi picked up the mugs and went to the kitchen while Dhaani sat there for a while, waiting for Shivi to break her silence.

A few minutes later, Shivi returned and began talking about the weather, the rain, and the soil. Dhaani let her have her time. Then Shivi said, "Sam loves rain too. I'm sure he'd be sitting in his swing and enjoying the view at this moment." She took a deep breath as if gaining self-composure amidst the rush of emotions.

Dhaani smilingly said, "Shivi, it's totally fine to talk about whatever is going on in your mind. Don't hesitate. Just share it with me."

"Yes, I thought about him last night. Rather, I thought about us. I absorbed all that you had explained to me and realised that you were right. Rose's brief stint doesn't make me a second choice at all."

"I'm glad you thought about it."

"Sammy and I have been friends for so long that we know each other inside and out. I had unrequited feelings, which I didn't even pay attention to. This proposal from Sam actually rubbed salt in those wounds accidentally. It isn't his fault. Perhaps I was carrying a burden inside my head. I had buried it so deep. Still, I'm glad it couldn't weigh down our friendship. I shall meet Sammy today and share my thoughts with him."

Dhaani hugged Shivi and patted her head, as she was happy and relieved that she could help Shivi bring her thought process on track.

If two souls can unite for a brilliant future,

Why not guide them to that juncture?

It's all a part of this beautiful social life that we live.

Just some forethought refines

The advice that we give.

Chapter 13

It Is Harder Than Expected

It was finally the time for new beginnings. Shivi met Sam. This meeting was a serious one—quite different from their regular talks. It was a genuine, mature talk based on the realisation, the guilt, and the acceptance of feelings from Sam and then from Shivi. Their friends had played a major role in laying the foundation for this moment. Both had clarity of intention, and their attitude was comforting towards each other. In a matter of twenty minutes, they ended up being a couple for life, who were yet to fall in love.

Once Shivi came back, the first thing that she did was to call up her mother. Her daily phone call to her mother used to be at night, so her mother got anxious and asked, "Is Sargam all right? You are calling early today!"

Those days, issues about Sargam not complying with Shivi's strictness were the general topics of discussion. Her mother thought maybe Sargam had created some fresh problems.

Shivi reassuringly said, "She's fine. Don't worry."

"Thank God. So, tell me what else is bothering you."

"Nothing is bothering me, Mummy. I wish to share something with you." After a pause, she added, "Sam almost proposed to me a few days ago. Initially, I didn't find it to be a good proposition. However, after thinking about it, I felt I was wrong. So, we met and talked today. We both feel that since we're great friends and know each other well, we can think along these lines."

"Are you listening, Mummy?"

"Yes, my child. I'm listening." Her voice had notes of excitement, and she became sentimental.

"Are you crying? Come on, Mummy!"

"No, I'm just elated. Tell me more about it."

Shivi laughed and said, "Okay, so we've planned to talk to our parents first, because we both are like that, and you people are our top priority." After a pause, she continued, "If both sides are okay, then we can arrange for all of us to meet and discuss further plans—marriage plans!" These words had notes of shyness, though.

"Shivi, I'm so happy to hear this. Your father would be on cloud nine to know that you want to get married. As far as the groom is concerned, we believe in your choice. Although we've not interacted much with Sam, the amount of help that he offered when you needed support with Sargam's tantrums revealed a lot about his personality. Whenever he's talked to us over the phone, he's come across as a very pleasant and mature person."

"Mummy, I'm glad to hear that. I wish that Dad also feels the same way."

"Of course he does! You wouldn't believe it if I told you that he even asked me a couple of times if you were thinking about marriage."

That evening, while Sargam was returning home, a dog bit her and badly injured her. With a blood-stained, mud-soaked t-shirt, she entered home. Shivi was shocked, and as soon as she came to know about the incident, she cleaned Sargam's wound. Later, she took her to the hospital to get vaccinated. Sargam had fallen so badly when the dog attacked her that her ankle got swollen. The doctor advised an X-ray too. However, there was no fracture detected on investigation, and they returned after getting the shot.

The next morning, when Shivi and Sargam talked to the parents, Shivi's father mentioned Sam and asked, "Has Sam talked to his mother? Have you both decided on something?"

Hearing this, Sargam was surprised and interjected, "Decided what?"

Shivi exclaimed, "Oh! How did I forget to tell you about it?"

"What is it?" asked Sargam.

"Sam and I wish to get married, and we want to get the family together for further planning."

"What? Marriage?"

Sargam got up from her chair and stomped angrily. She said, "How could you?"

"Sargam, you're acting weird. We forgot to tell you. It's just been twelve hours since I told Mummy about it!"

"You are so smart—so cunning! You impose so many restrictions on me and are enjoying an affair yourself."

"Sargam!" shouted Shivi. She told her parents that she would call them in another ten minutes and then ended the call.

Shivi angrily said to her sister, "Are you out of your mind? We're mature adults, and there wasn't any affair. Oh, why am I even explaining this to you? You are a teenager, and it's my duty to ensure that you stay on the right track. You pay attention to all irrelevant things other than your studies. That is why you face restrictions."

"I know! I know everything," said Sargam and she walked away towards her room.

"Listen to me," said Shivi. Pulling Sargam by her arm, Shivi stopped her and said, "It slipped my mind because you got a dog bite. Your well-being became my priority."

"Wow, now you have many reasons," said Sargam.

This unruly and unwarranted attitude from Sargam was enough for Shivi to adopt silence for the rest of the evening.

It took a couple of days for the girls to get back to normal. Two weeks later, Sargam finished her exams, and Sam and Shivi decided to call their parents to Delhi so that they could meet.

Shivi's parents came to Delhi by themselves, while Sam went to bring his mother along.

The parents met, and it was a very nice, lively meeting at Shivi's place. Then Sam took everyone for an outing to show them around Connaught Place. At night, Sam and Shivi planned a dinner at a three-star hotel in the city's heart. The next day, Shivi took the ladies out for boating at The Red Fort in the morning. Sargam stayed back as she wasn't feeling well. She had a headache when her mother returned, so she requested her to massage some hot oil on her head. She seemed emotional as the parents were to leave the next morning. She said to her mother in a sombre tone, "I want you to stay longer. I miss you so much here. I feel extremely lonely sometimes."

"Why should you feel lonely? Your elder sister is here, and she takes good care of you."

"She does, but I miss you. She loves me but scolds me even more."

Sargam teared up, and her mother asked, "What is the matter? Why are you crying? Does your head hurt so much? Do you need any medicine?"

"No, Mummy. I'm just a bit overwhelmed. No doubt, she takes care of me, but sometimes she makes such childish decisions that I feel I'm more mature than her."

"What are you saying, Sargam? What childish decisions are you talking about?"

"For me, she has such strict rules. She doesn't approve of me talking to strangers or going out with male friends. She has a problem with me talking on the phone. She complains that I spend hours on the phone and applies no critical logic to her own self."

"Sargam, she's older than you and has taken up your responsibility. She needs to be strict sometimes. Like we take care of her, she cares for you."

"But you never stopped her from meeting Sam or going out with him. She had it so easy—she just informed you, and you readily agreed. You never asked about Sam's family or his background. I bet you don't even plan to ask her anything of that sort."

"Why are you saying such bitter things?"

"No, it's not at all bitter. It's the truth. This is going to be an inter-caste, inter-religion, inter-state marriage—but no one paid attention to all of that. You people just agreed to what she told you. In the village, no one would have approved of it."

"Sargam, you seem to be annoyed with your sister for some stupid reason. Let me tell you, we are doing our duties very well. We have talked to her about everything. In fact, she sought permission from us—she has not thrust her decision on us!"

"Mummy, don't be so critical of my view. I'm not annoyed with her. I'm just putting forth my thoughts. You tell me, if Sam's family followed the same religion as us, couldn't we all have visited the temple together yesterday afternoon? They didn't come. Instead, they went to his mother's friend's place and spent time there. Shivi and Sam didn't even reveal details about the wedding—the rituals—and the style in which it's going to take place! I'm just comparing her attitude as a guardian to yours."

Her mother took a pause and said, "Ok, I won't stop you. You can tell me all your thoughts."

Sargam poured her heart out. The mother listened to all of it patiently and authoritatively explained to Sargam that she needn't worry.

She said, "We believe that Sam and Shivi will figure everything out. Mrs. Fernandes is a very down-to-earth, open-minded, and helpful lady. You'll learn about these things when you grow up a bit more. Just analysing some slight gestures can help one guess some things in the blink of an eye. Didn't you see how she met us—no arrogance, no airs! She has such a caring attitude towards Shivi, and only a mother can make that out; you are too young to catch those points. Mothers-in-law can be so much trouble; there are people who change stances every minute. Mrs. Fernandes firmly supported her son in each of his decisions. You don't need to worry. No background check is required for Sam. Shivi has known him for so long. I'm sure she knows what she's doing."

Her mother had tried to convince and comfort Sargam about the rightness of Shivi's decision. To what extent Sargam had absorbed those points of wisdom was a million-dollar question.

A month later, Shivi and Sam put in applications for leave to go ahead with their wedding. Surprisingly, there was no reason for it, but their leave applications were rejected. Both were at the Connaught Place branch now, and there was no way Ranjan or his team members could have known about it. This surprised Sam. Shivi also felt disheartened and told her mother about it over a call. Except Sargam, all felt sad. Maybe always being at loggerheads with Shivi made her react unreasonably coolly. She told Shivi straight away that they should postpone the wedding for some more months until the company approved their leave. Shivi and Sam were too sad to even pay attention to how Sargam had reacted.

A few more months passed, and things at their office began getting messier suddenly. A few interns on Shivi's team complained of negligence on her part. They alleged that she was hand in glove with the senior employees harassing them, as she didn't address their grievances. They complained of mistreatment at the hands of a store manager, who was a day-one employee of Seva Troop. Shivi investigated the complaints from the interns, who had also said that the store manager looked down upon them and did not give them access to some crucial files. She talked to the store manager, but he ignored her concern and continued to behave in his usual manner. Unfortunately, he was loyal to Ranjan and listened to his commands despite being at a different office. She highlighted this issue in managerial meetings. However, the issue remained unsolved, and the onus of the resultant misunderstanding came on her. Ranjan could thus create this divide between Shivi and her interns. Eventually, there was distrust, and her year-end reports bore the brunt.

Sam's appraisals got messed up, too. He had always been someone who promoted his team over himself. His immediate boss took advantage of his helpfulness. He took credit for the success of all the projects that Sam had handled. He piled work on Sam by sending him out of the city right before a couple of high-level management meetings, and thus, he took all the credit. It was like a walk in the park for him. At this time, things were not working out well for Sam at all.

The company held back Shivi's bonus. Sam's boss told him that his performance did not meet expectations. Their morale was low. They were being blamed and targeted for not performing, even when the requirements from their immediate bosses were pretty unclear. They felt that this resulted from the induction of relatives of top management in the company, and it was an effort to make a place for those people. It was as if Seva Troop was losing its charm. Office politics was taking evil turns. It was jeopardising the work culture at Seva Troop. Earlier Ranjan was the sole source of unpleasantness but now it was coming from all quarters. They weren't feeling valued, and every day, an additional issue was cropping up. The environment was becoming toxic day by day, and they were having trouble navigating through it all. Consequently, their workload doubled, and they didn't even have time to scratch their heads. As time wasn't permitting them to have a wedding celebration, Shivi and Sam decided on a registered marriage as a last resort.

After six months, their parents arrived in Delhi. It was three days before the date of the wedding registration. Shivi's mother, Mrs. Singh, had instructed her to hide the date from Sargam. She had told Shivi that they would surprise Sargam with the news after her exams, as otherwise, she'd throw tantrums and dissipate money on dresses and jewellery. Shivi initially resisted her mother's idea of hiding the information from Sargam. Her mother convinced her, saying that she'd handle it. She told Shivi that she wanted Sargam to concentrate on her studies. Shivi eventually followed her mother's advice.

On Friday afternoon, when Sargam came home after taking an examination, she was surprised. Elated to see her parents, she giggled and jumped. However, her excitement was short-lived. As expected, there was a lot of discussion about why they had kept her in the dark. Unusually disturbed and annoyed, she even resented going for the wedding registration and had to be forced by her mother to accompany them to the Registrar's office. It was important to note that her mother took charge of handling Sargam's unruly attitude. Maybe Mrs. Singh had something in her mind that she didn't share with anyone. Maybe she was trying to keep things simple for Shivi.

At the Registrar's office, Sam and Shivi signed the papers and then exchanged beautiful garlands that Mrs. Fernandes had lovingly made using fragrant pink roses and pearls. The garlands had intricate gold lace bows in the centre to signify the light that Sam and Shivi carried as a couple. Shivi's parents gifted the couple gold bands with their names etched alongside the date of their wedding. Then they exchanged the rings. Sam hugged Shivi and kissed her on the forehead. Shivi's happy tears told a story of how grateful and blessed she felt to have Sam as a life partner. Later, they all went for lunch to the couple's favourite restaurant. There, they cut a cake amidst a shower of rose petals.

Just the next day after their marriage, Sam and Shivi resumed office, as the audit season was around the corner. They took along a box of sweets and revealed the news to their colleagues. A cosy celebration followed in the office canteen itself.

Two days later, Sam was informed in a meeting that he was being transferred to the East Delhi branch. He immediately understood that Ranjan had a role to play in this move. He was expecting such fireworks, especially after his marriage. When he checked with his trusted sources, it became known that Ranjan wanted to swap positions with Sam. However, Sam was clever enough to offer his resignation instead of accepting the transfer. He knew he was too valuable for the company to lose, as the new recruits didn't have the potential to perform well and the management had gradually understood this. As expected, the transfer didn't happen.

Ranjan was hopping mad now. Since he could not harm Sam or Shivi, he made Vivaan his target. As a part of another surprise rejig, Vivaan had to move to the East Delhi branch, and two months later, Vivaan and Ranjan had a fierce clash. It so happened that Vivaan got to know about the misappropriation of company funds by Ranjan and his team. He declared that he'd report it. Consequently, Ranjan threatened him and fearlessly told him to mind his own business. Vivaan retaliated and wrote to higher authorities. Ranjan came to know about it and warned him upfront, by saying, "What do you think of yourself? You are just a small fish here and I'm the whale. You won't even know when I'll eliminate you from this game."

A furious Vivaan retorted, "Do whatever you can. I'm right, and I know it. You and your team have brought enough disrepute to Seva Troop."

"Who cares! Be on the lookout for another job."

"Let's see whose job is in trouble," said Vivaan.

The discussion was getting intense. In a fit of rage, Ranjan caught Vivaan's collar and said, "Do you remember the attack on Sam and Shivi? Be ready!"

Vivaan couldn't believe what he had just heard. Ranjan soon left the room. Vivaan immediately shared it with Sam over a call. Sam told him to report the matter to the management. However, Vivaan's appeal fell on deaf ears because Ranjan already had his nexus in the management to sort matters out in his favour.

Vivaan eventually left Seva Troop and later got busy attending coaching classes as he cleared the preliminary exams and had savings up his sleeve. Dhaani was already on the lookout for a lighter job, so she joined an NGO that worked for the welfare of underprivileged children.

Shivi and Sam had now begun thinking about changing their job because of purposeful separations arising out of office politics. One day, they were having a conversation about this issue when Shivi said to Sam, "Dhaani has told me that there's a vacancy that matches my profile at her office."

"So, what are you waiting for? You should apply."

"Sammy, the thing is that whatever the situation may be, the truth remains that here, at Seva Troop, we are together."

"Are we even together? Ranjan's nexus is widespread, and he ensures that we never go on the same distribution drive. Instead, most of the time, you are on the roster for night-time duties."

"But at least you accompany me, even if it's an off-duty task for you!"

"Oh yes, and I'm not complaining. It's my duty to protect you. I can't leave you alone even if it amounts to putting in extra hours following you on your night-time duties."

"I'm blessed to have you. Things really become difficult when I'm asked to go for unnecessary training in Chandigarh. I have to manage it alone there. However, you've trained me well to handle Ranjan's immoral advances."

"Actually, when I think about changing this job, it has more to do with mental peace than anything else. Obviously, another job could have its own challenges, but it's the frustration from office politics which drives me to think about shifting."

"Apart from that, there's another concern that nags me, Sam. Our parents are ageing and at some point, they will need us more than ever. I wish we all lived closer so that we could take over those responsibilities. So, when I think of leaving Seva Troop, it has to be to move closer to our parents. I can't settle for anything less."

"I agree with you, Shivi. I actually feel blessed that you think along these lines."

At any point in life,

Do complications leave us alone?

Does life ever become as simple

In childhood as it was known?

Chapter 14

The Mishap at Nagpur

Shivi and Sam had been married for a year now. They had just returned from Nagpur after celebrating this milestone with Sam's mother and aunt. The next morning, Sam received a call from his mother, who was sounding very disturbed, "Your aunt has been down with fever and diarrhoea. She cannot take in a sip of water. The doctor has recommended getting her admitted to the hospital. I have called for an ambulance and shall take her to the medical facility nearby."

"It might be a severe infection needing prompt treatment. I'll apply for leave and will be there with you by the evening. Don't worry, Mom."

"Yes, Sam. I think you should come back. I know that you both just returned to Delhi, but she looks to be in awful shape, and I can't handle this alone."

Soon, Sam was on his flight to Nagpur. When he reached there, he got the sad news that his aunt had passed away an hour before his arrival. She had suffered multi-organ failure. Sombreness had spread its wings, and his mother was inconsolable. It was comforting for her to see Sam. As soon as he hugged her, she burst into tears. Over the next few days, they completed the rituals for his aunt's departed soul. Later, Sam half-heartedly went back to Delhi. He didn't want to leave his mother alone there, but she resisted shifting base as she felt comfortable in her own home.

Once Sam came to Delhi, he remained unsettled for a couple of weeks. He went back to look her up within a month's time. Although she was fine, he sensed that loneliness had descended in their house. He thought, *I better figure something out, so that she stays near me, and I can take care of her. Eventually, this gloomy environment is going to affect her mindset.*

One day, when he was visiting his mother on a weekend, he sat her down and said, "Mom, you need to be out of this place. I understand that it's your own house. I understand that you've made a life for yourself here. But, till the time Aunty was with you, things were fine. Now, you are alone. Your friends or, for that matter, friendly neighbours can't be with you twenty-four-seven. Everyone will eventually return to their schedule. There will be days when you would want someone to be with you, to talk to you, or maybe even cook for you."

"No, I am content with the way I am. I enjoy spending time with myself."

"Mom, it will not always be the same. Presently, you are in perfect health, but even if you get a mild flu, who will be by your side? I feel you need to be with us in Delhi. If it were possible, I would have left my job and settled here, but opportunities aren't available here. If I settle for a lower salary, we'll be living hand to mouth. There, Shivi and I get good salaries. You'll get your pension there, too.

So, why do you feel that you'll lose your independence? Why don't you shift and stay with us?"

"I don't want to be dependent on you. I don't want to go through any mess. You're married now. I know Shivi is a nice girl, and she values her relationships, but who knows, over time, she might not like the idea of me staying with both of you. Then, I'll have to shift back again because I can't spoil your life. Shivi's sister is already staying with you both."

"Mom, you are overthinking. As if you don't know about Shivi's nature!"

"No, these are the realities of life."

"Okay, what if I get you an apartment in my building?"

"Who will pay the hefty rent, Sam?"

"I'll pay the rent, Mom."

"No, that doesn't work for me. I'd rather be in this home. I'll manage by myself. You can visit me more often if you feel insecure."

He didn't want to force her, so he thought of trying another time. Shivi also kept convincing her to move to Delhi every time she could. Meanwhile, Sam and Shivi alternately began visiting her every two weeks.

One day, when Shivi and her mother-in-law were taking a stroll in the community park, a lady with grey hair stopped by and asked, "Is she your daughter-in-law, Mrs Fernandes? I'm meeting her for the first time."

Sam's mom replied, "Yes, she is Shivi, Sam's wife. Isn't she gorgeous?"

"Absolutely," replied the lady.

Then she caringly put her hand on Shivi's head and said, "Your mother-in-law keeps praising you all the time."

Shivi smiled, and her flushed face looked even prettier. The lady opened her wallet and pulled out a five-hundred-rupee note and handed it over to Shivi. She said to Shivi, "Buy yourself something nice."

Shivi thanked the old lady for the gift and gave her a tight hug. At night, when Shivi was preparing food in the kitchen, her mother-in-law said, "Shivi, I don't feel like having home-cooked food. Let's order something from the restaurant nearby."

Shivi replied, "Mummy, you have been so unwell in the past week, and still, you want to eat food from outside. Nothing doing! I'm making a nice vegetable stew and some boiled rice to go with it."

After a minute, Shivi added, "At the maximum, I can let you have some poppadom and pickle with this. Believe me, you'll love the meal. Sam has told me to take care of your diet."

"Okay, as you say."

Suddenly, a loud sound came from the kitchen, as if something had exploded. Mrs. Fernandes ran towards the kitchen and saw an exploded pressure cooker. Bits of carrots, peas, and tomatoes had splashed onto the walls. She screamed for Shivi. Thankfully, Shivi had just left the kitchen a few seconds ago and had gone into the washroom. Shivi rushed out, and as soon as she saw her mother-in-law standing there, she exclaimed, "Oh, my God! What happened?"

Her mother-in-law turned around and hugged her. Guilt overpowered Shivi. She had tears in her eyes, as she thought she must have faltered. Her mother-in-law, however, was relieved that Shivi was safe. She calmed her down, and that was their moment—a perfect mother-daughter moment!

Mrs Fernandes kissed Shivi's face and forehead over and over, saying, "Oh, my daughter! Just don't worry, we're fine, we're absolutely fine, God is great! Stop crying, my child."

Shivi said, "Sorry. I don't know why this happened. I must have made some mistake while closing the cooker."

"No, my darling. Don't say that."

She caressed Shivi and told her to relax. After half an hour, when both had returned to normalcy, they made jam sandwiches and tea. Later, they slept.

Shivi was supposed to leave a day later, so her mother-in-law took her out for shopping. At the store, Shivi got uncomfortable, as the salesperson who was draping the saree on Shivi tried to misbehave with her. Her mother-in-law was so watchful that even before Shivi could react, she got up from her chair and slapped the miscreant. There was a commotion as the shop owner tried to defend the salesperson, who was crying foul. Soon, Shivi called the police, and they got hold of the CCTV footage and the man admitted his fault. Later that night, to lighten the mood, Mrs. Fernandes opened her box of heritage sarees. Shivi spent the night trying on a few handpicked ones and ended up taking four of them, along with her, to Delhi. They both surely developed an amazing bond during this time.

It had barely been six months since Sam had lost his aunt when Shivi also received terrible news. Her father passed away due to a cardiac arrest. Shivi, Sam, and Sargam rushed to Himachal Pradesh. Mr Singh, Shivi's father, had been hale and hearty and hadn't had any health issues earlier, so this was a shock for the family. Once the post-death rituals were over, Sam asked his mother-in-law how this had happened. She told him, "A week ago, one day, when he came home from work, he told me he was feeling uneasy. Thinking it must be acidity causing the discomfort, I gave him buttermilk. The pain in his chest subsided after drinking it. I told him to visit a medical facility for a check-up, but he refused. On Sunday, when he woke up in the morning, he didn't complain of any pain. He was feeling absolutely fine. After breakfast, he got up from his chair and suddenly collapsed."

"Was he stressed?" asked Sam.

"No, stress didn't affect him. He was always very strong."

One of her father's friends gestured for Shivi to come outside. She followed him, and he told her, "Your mother is trying to be strong. She is hiding the fact that your father was under tremendous pressure from the village sarpanch to leave this place."

"Leave this place! But why?"

"Since the time people in the village came to know that you had got married outside the community, the pressure to oust your parents from the community had been building up."

"What? She didn't tell me anything."

"Yes, I know. They didn't want to bother you. The community had distanced themselves from your parents to a great extent. That is the reason there is nobody at your home today other than family members. Otherwise, the entire village would have been here."

Shivi thanked her uncle for telling her the truth. She went inside. Subsequently, she talked to Sam about it.

On listening to all that Shivi told him, Sam said, "So, this means we cannot afford to leave Mrs. Singh alone here."

"Yes, you're absolutely right."

"We must take her to Delhi."

"She won't agree to that."

"Then, either you or Sargam would have to stay with her until she agrees to come to Delhi."

"I'll stay with her. Sargam has exams this week. Moreover, I don't know how Sargam would react if something goes wrong. She is a hothead. There are troublemakers in the village, and we can't deny that. I don't feel that she is mature enough to handle things."

Shivi took a week off from work and stayed with her mother. Sargam returned to Delhi with Sam, and then Sam went to Chandigarh for four days for work. When one of her cousins came from a neighbouring village to stay with her mother for a month, Shivi returned to Delhi.

Circumstances control us

No matter how strong

We portray ourselves to be!

A single flick from destiny

Shows us how prepared we are

Against the waves at the sea.

Chapter 15

Mrs. Singh and Mrs. Fernandes Shift Base

Since both Mrs. Fernandes and Mrs. Singh were alone now and in two different cities, it was becoming difficult for Sam and Shivi to look after them. They both kept on convincing the ladies to shift with them to Delhi, but both resisted. One day, when Shivi was in Himachal Pradesh, and Sam was in Nagpur, Sargam fell terribly ill in Delhi. She had to be admitted to a hospital by her friends. She had caught a severe intestinal infection and became dehydrated. There was total chaos, as none of the family members could be with her. On this day, Mrs. Singh realised Shivi and Sam's plight. She could understand what they had been going through in the past few months. She told Shivi that she would shift to Delhi if Sam's mother also agreed to do so!

This was the most comforting thing that Shivi had heard in a while. She was proud of her mother for being gracious enough to think compassionately about Sam's mom. Shivi immediately rang up Sam and told him about it. Sam was on cloud nine because he had never thought this would happen. He talked to his mother immediately. Later, even Mrs Singh talked to her to convince her. Things worked out, and Mrs Fernandes also agreed to shift permanently to Delhi. It was an enormous relief for the couple, as they had been trying to accomplish this for a long time.

Sam decided to rent an apartment nearby because both the ladies had agreed to stay together. Soon, he found a flat in the same building as his.

A couple of weeks later, both Sam's and Shivi's mothers arrived in Delhi. Shivi and Sam had already set up the house for them. This was the first time that Mrs. Singh and Mrs. Fernandes were going to be in each other's company twenty-four-seven, so there were obvious jitters that Shivi experienced. One day, she anxiously said to Sam, "We've planned everything and made all the arrangements. I just hope they get along well because the only time that they've spent together was during our wedding. Although we know they are very adjusting ladies, the fact that they are co-mothers-in-law may still create some trouble. I hope that does not happen."

"Oh, Shivi. You don't have to worry so much. Neither of them has ego issues. They are simple, understanding, and very mature ladies. Their agreeing to the proposal is enough of an assurance that they understand the situation."

"Yes, I think you're right. But you know what disturbs me? This is a metropolitan city and the society here is different. The old ladies in our colony are intrusive and inquisitive! Our moms are simple—too simple for them."

"Don't worry. It'll all be fine."

"I hope so," said Shivi.

A few days went by. Now, Sam and Shivi spent most of the evenings in the company of their mothers, with Sargam joining them occasionally. She used to be busy with her friends most of the time. Taking care of their family in their time of need was a great feeling for the couple. Often, they all went out for lunch on weekends. Sam ensured that the older adults stayed excited about the new place because he knew they'd be missing their respective homes. Shivi made it a point to have tea with them in the evening after returning from the office. They all used to dine together, even when Sam was out of town for work.

After a month of having settled in, Mrs Singh thought of getting Sargam to move in with her. One day, she said to Sargam, "Now that your exams are over, you must pack up your belongings and vacate your room. Move in upstairs with us."

"Move in! Why should I?"

"Because I'm staying here; you're supposed to stay with me, and not at your sister's place!"

"No way. I'm not moving anywhere. Don't even think about it, Mummy."

"Sargam, I'm not asking you. I'm telling you! You'd better pack up your stuff and move. Shivi and Sam have done enough for you. It's not their duty anymore."

"Nobody is doing me any favours. I help Shivi with household chores. I do my laundry." She paused for a moment and asked, "Wait a minute—did Shivi tell you to say all this to me? Because I'm sure Sam would never say this."

"No, nobody has said anything."

Sargam was angry and she exited the room.

The next day, they were all having tea when Sargam entered the house and, saying nothing, went straight to her room. Shivi seemed confused. Mrs. Fernandes was also there. Sargam's behaviour embarrassed Mrs. Singh. So, Mrs. Singh called her out, but she replied from her room, saying that she wasn't feeling well. Sensing that the atmosphere of the house might turn tense at any moment, Sam requested Mrs. Singh to calm down. His mother seconded his view.

Mrs Singh took Shivi into confidence the next day and asked her some detailed questions about Sargam's behaviour at home. She said to Shivi, "I have noticed that Sargam behaves weirdly sometimes. She ought to have respect for Sam. Seems like she still treats him like a friend. I hope she never disrespects you people."

"With Sam, her behaviour is fine. However, she answers me back most of the time. Often, I feel like giving her a piece of my mind, but Sam advises me to avoid any arguments. She completely changes her tone in front of Sam. It is so embarrassing for me, but thankfully, Sam understands my emotions and her behaviour too. He handles these situations very well."

"I have been seeing that. Don't worry. Now that I'm here, I'll ensure that she stays within her limits."

"But don't make it obvious, Mummy. She will react badly."

"I know her inside out. First, I'll get her to shift upstairs with me. Now that I've shifted to Delhi, there's no reason for her to stay downstairs with you and Sam. Then I'll counsel her about respecting relations."

"Oh, Mummy! I thought that I'd talk to you about it. But Sam cautioned me against it because he wanted you and Mrs. Fernandes to get settled peacefully first."

"Oh! We're already settled. Your mother-in-law is such a gem of a person. She is very accommodating. She never complains about anything. Initially, I was hesitant when we actually moved in. I was sceptical about how I would stay with her because I've spent my entire life in the village. But the very first day, she told me I should consider her my friend. She explained how she had been living happily with her sister-in-law for so many years. Her tone is so welcoming. She has an immensely warm nature."

"Yes, she is indeed very warm. I'm glad that this has finally happened. At least Sam and I are at peace, thinking we'll be able to care for you both in your golden years."

Shivi hugged her mother and felt much more comfortable after their heart-to-heart talk.

Afterwards, another time around, Mrs. Singh asked Sargam to shift upstairs with her, but she didn't take it very well. So, Mrs. Singh thought of talking to Sam about it. One evening, she sat down with Shivi and Sam for tea and said to them, "I'm very disturbed at Sargam's refusal to move in with me. I'm trying to get her to do so, but she refuses outright. I'm pretty sure she won't listen to Shivi either."

Sam said, "You do not have to worry about it. It's fine. She's like a child to us."

Mrs. Singh told him, "No, Sam. It isn't fine at all. She is an adult and needs to respect her elders. I feel so embarrassed about the fact that she is living with both of you. I shouldn't be saying this, but Sargam shows some mixed emotions. I'm not doubting her intentions, but I do sense something fishy. You are a son to me, and I have no qualms in revealing my deepest and embarrassing fears to you."

Sam got up from his chair. He went and sat beside Mrs Singh and said to her, "Oh, Mom. You're getting stressed. It's just nothing. Maybe she's refusing because my mother also stays in the same house. She might be feeling uncomfortable. Often, teenagers behave this way."

Mrs. Singh nodded in disapproval. Sam continued to convince her that she should take it easy.

A couple of months passed. Sargam was now in the last year of her course at college. One evening, she consulted Sam for guidance. She asked him, "I'm looking for internship opportunities. Can you guide me on this?"

"Of course, Sargam. It is a step in the right direction, as a good internship gives the required push to one's career. You must look for a company with a proven track record and a positive reputation for its work culture."

"How about applying to Seva Troop for an internship? You can help me get in, right?"

"Of course I can, but I feel you should explore a few more companies too. Try to secure a spot for yourself at a multinational company first. It shall hold more value."

"Yes, I'll be doing that. Several friends and batchmates of mine are trying for the top companies in Delhi. Our professors are also helping them by connecting them with their former pupils who are working in those firms."

It was a healthy discussion. Sargam agreed to look for opportunities. Later that night, Sam told Shivi about it. Shivi was surprised and asked, "How did she come to know that Seva Troop offers internships? I never told her anything about it because I knew she would like to take the simpler route. Did you tell her that there are spots for an internship at our office?"

"No, I didn't. I thought you'd have said something."

"Not at all. I'm worried. I hope she isn't in touch with Ranjan!"

"How can that be? You're overthinking. Maybe she asked without knowing about the spots being available at the company. She could have got information from her college."

"I don't think that's possible because we've never had students interning from her college at Seva Troop."

Just then, Sam got a call from Vivaan, and he got busy talking. Shivi was tired, so she slept.

Sargam wished to take advantage of Sam's and Shivi's positions at Seva Troop. She didn't seem to be ready to put in effort for herself. Sam could very well foresee that it was going to turn into a major issue in the future.

A week went by. One day, Sam asked Sargam, "So, what about your internship applications? Where have you sent requests?"

"Not yet. I'm still thinking about where to send my applications."

"Why so? I thought that you'd have applied by now."

"Actually, I'm waiting for my friend. She has a cousin who works for a multinational company, and there is a better scope there. He has promised us two spots."

"Sargam, that isn't the way! You should not be looking for favours right at the start of your career. You must apply at least. Worst comes to worst, they'll reject your application. At least you'll learn to go through the process. Otherwise, how will you learn about the way professional institutions work?"

"Okay, I'll apply tomorrow. I had already shortlisted a few companies, but was just waiting because of my friend."

A month went by, and she didn't get a response from any of the places that she had applied to. Her friend's cousin also turned a deaf ear because he himself got fired. So, Sargam requested Sam and Shivi to get her a spot for an internship at Seva Troop, and they yielded because it was the last day to apply.

Soon, Sargam joined the office. This day was Sargam's first as an intern at Seva Troop. She had nine other students with her. The organisers grouped them into two teams. One team was headed by Sam's reporting manager and the other was under Shivi. Sargam got to train under Shivi.

The first day was fine. However, on the second day, Sargam went to Sam's cabin after lunch and said that she wanted him to change her team. Sam was shocked. He told her that this was not their home, where she could complain about every little thing to him. Howling, she said, "Shivi is bossy. She treats me like she's the principal of a school and I'm a nursery student! She scolded me so badly in front of all the apprentices today. I felt so humiliated."

"And why was it so?"

"I didn't address her as Ma'am."

"She's absolutely right, then. Sargam, your behaviour isn't proper. You are in a professional setup, and you need to behave accordingly. There are some rules which you are supposed to follow."

"But I'm not comfortable being on her team. I won't be able to learn anything there."

"Sargam, I cannot help you with this because this is against the company's policy. A lottery system was used to create the teams, as we had declared that you were a relative. It was a decision made by the management. You should be happy that she is your supervisor. Believe me, even the fact that you got a place in her team was a pleasant surprise for both of us. You should be grateful. You do not know how supervisors can be!"

"I wanted to learn from you."

"What are you saying, Sargam? This isn't how things work in a corporate setting. Please follow the instructions if you actually want to learn something and set up a sound foundation."

Sam's tone was harsh, and Sargam left his cabin in a fit of rage.

Subsequently, Sargam began interfering in Shivi's work. She left no stone unturned to damage Shivi's reputation at the office. She supported unworthy ideas from other teams and never appreciated Shivi's ideas. Even during lunchtime discussions among peers, she criticised her own sister. She badmouthed Shivi in every way she could. One of Shivi's interns came to Shivi and talked to her about it. Shivi never expected that Sargam would stoop down to such lows. She knew Sargam had a few bones to pick with her, but she never thought Sargam would behave in such a manner. Sam was also angry when he got to know about it. Sargam complained about some issues to her peers who were on the other team, and they conveyed it all to their leader. Sargam was indulging in gossip and spoiling the organisational environment. When it was becoming too much, Sam instructed her forthrightly to talk to her team lead first. However, she wasn't yielding. When all her tricks failed, she even sneakily misfiled entries in a task given to her by Shivi. Shivi was so occupied that she came to know about it only during a presentation. Shivi had to apologise to the management. She knew it was Sargam's doing. She and Sam asked her about it, but Sargam refused to accept her wrongdoing.

Thanks to Sargam, Shivi's troubles extended much beyond the office. Sargam behaved childishly and always sat in the front seat of the car when all three of them used to head back home. Shivi felt weird, but Sam, being the strong pillar of the family, tolerated those small things. He wanted to maintain peace within the family. After six months, when the apprenticeship finally ended, Shivi heaved a sigh of relief. Sargam's presence at the office had been a pain in the neck for her. However, she tried to take all of it in her stride, as she knew about Sargam's nature very well.

Time passed, and it was New Year's Eve. Sam and Shivi had planned to go for a dance night at a hotel with their group of friends. While Shivi was getting ready, she suddenly felt lightheaded—breathless, to say the least—and Sam noticed it. She brushed it off as weakness while Sam was concerned. Sam said, "Let's cancel the plan. There'll be glaring lights all around and loud music, too. The hall is going to be crowded. If you aren't feeling well, it isn't a good idea to go to the party."

"No, Sammy. I want to go. Once we're there, I'll forget all of this, and I just want to enjoy and relax. It's been a long time since we both went out together."

Sargam entered the room just then and said, "Hey, are both of you going out partying tonight?"

"Yes, dear," replied Shivi.

Sam intervened and said, "She doesn't seem to be very well. I feel like cancelling the plan; however, she's insisting on going there."

Sargam instantly said, "He's absolutely right. If you're not feeling well, you shouldn't go."

Shivi looked at Sam and said, "You're exaggerating; I'm okay. Get ready, Sam. We're already late!"

Sargam inched towards Shivi and said, "You look so tired. I would say that you get some rest. Otherwise, you'll wake up feeling lazy on the very first day of the year."

By this time, Sam had opened his wardrobe and began selecting clothes.

Shivi held Sargam's arms, turned her around forcefully, and said, "Sargam, Sam has to get ready. I've prepared a sumptuous dinner. Come, let me show it to you. You'll have to heat it up before eating. Serve it on time because both Mummy and Sam's mummy need to take their sleep medication after dinner."

She forcefully took Sargam to the kitchen. Later, Shivi and Sam left for the party.

While they were in the car heading towards the hotel, Shivi seemed uncomfortable. Sam asked her, "Are you okay?"

"Yes, I'm fine."

"You seem a bit lost!"

"Yes, I am thinking about something."

"What is it, Shivi?"

"Sargam."

Sam smiled and put his hand on hers reassuringly. Then he said, "Just ignore it, Shivi."

"Sometimes, I just can't help it! She is my sister. Things become so complicated."

"We've had this discussion before, my dear. Just ignore it. Enjoy your New Year's Eve."

"Yes, you're right. We've had this discussion a million times. I don't know when she will understand that she needs to respect our privacy. She just barges into our room whenever she pleases. I don't like it. Often, I feel she crosses her limits and engages you in prolonged personal talk. She shouldn't be talking about romantic movies with you. Should she?"

Sam laughed and said, "Shivi, she's like a child to me."

"I know that. But there has to be a limit. Mummy is so tired of trying to get her to shift upstairs. It's only you who takes her side every time. I just don't know how you do it!"

Shivi put her left hand over Sam's and gave him a contented smile. They reached the venue. As soon as Shivi disembarked, a car zoomed past her. Shivi was shocked and said, "Had I been a few inches to the right, I wouldn't have been alive."

"Don't say that, Shivi!"

"I don't understand why someone would drive so close to the side on a wide road, and that too so well-lit up. I hope someone's not trying to harm me."

"You mean Ranjan? You don't need to be so scared. He knows we are vigilant."

"Who knows? I've been getting blank calls for the last week. Remember, I told you."

"It can't be Ranjan. He has nothing to do with us now. He is in trouble himself."

The conversation ended there, and they proceeded to the ballroom of the hotel. They spent a couple of hours grooving to the music. A little after the clock struck twelve, they left for home. When they returned, they came to know that Mrs. Singh had slipped down the stairs and had fractured her leg. Sargam had taken her to the hospital, and the doctor plastered Mrs. Singh's leg. Interestingly, Mrs. Singh had seized the opportunity to get Sargam to shift upstairs with her. Sargam had no choice and couldn't refuse this move. Though seeing her mother with a plastered leg was painful for Shivi, she knew that healing was near. It was more of a relief for Shivi and her mother because Sargam was finally out of Shivi's house. Seeing the larger picture, they both got mental peace.

After a couple of months, one day, the four friends met for lunch. Shivi and Sam were in a better frame of mind after a long time because of situations getting settled, both at the office and at home. Dhaani and Vivaan were now preparing for their last attempt at the civil services examination. Sam and Shivi shared with them the changes that had taken place in Seva Troop. In a breath of fresh air, a long-overdue overhaul at the managerial level had finally taken effect. The committee for women's welfare had noticed grey areas, and on their recommendation, the management had reshuffled the teams. As a result, Ranjan got a tit-for-tat treatment. His favourite co-workers were put on different projects, and some were even shifted to the new offices of Seva Troop in Himachal Pradesh and Punjab. Ranjan now had no means left to accomplish his evil doings. No more could he siphon off funds from the company for personal use too.

A few days later, when the family was together at the tea table one evening, Sargam told everyone that she had secured a job. Sam sought details from her about the company. She happily provided the same. He became concerned and remarked that he hadn't heard about the company. He asked why she had not consulted him or Shivi before accepting the offer. She replied that it was because she wanted to surprise everyone. Her mother was happy that now Sargam would also be on her own. However, Shivi and Sam were sceptical about this job of hers.

Two months flew by. One evening, Sargam's mother asked her about her first salary. Sargam said that she had yet to receive it, as the company had a policy of paying new employees two months after joining. Mrs. Singh found it strange and talked to Shivi, who then talked to Sam about it. Since Sargam had never been the child who followed the rules, they wished to cross-check with her company. When Sam could not find her name on the company's roll, he confronted Sargam with the facts. She countered by saying that she was still a trainee and hadn't been officially inducted yet. Sam got suspicious and enquired from his friends if anyone knew someone who worked for that firm. He wanted to ensure that Sargam was safe and on the right track.

A few days later, one of Sam's contacts confirmed Sargam wasn't working for that company. Sam got angry and told Shivi to ask Sargam about what was going on. Shivi skipped asking Sargam questions. Instead, she resolved to uncover the truth herself. Subsequently, she followed Sargam a couple of times but lost sight of her in the traffic and failed in her investigation.

One day, Shivi went out shopping. She wanted to purchase a mobile phone for Sam as his birthday was approaching. When she selected the phone and was about to make the payment, she realised that the money from her purse was missing. Shocked, she returned home. She talked to Sam about it that evening. She said, "I'm very disturbed. I lost twenty thousand rupees today."

"How come?" asked Sam.

"I took the money from the cupboard and went to the market. I wanted to buy a phone for you. I had to make the payment at the store, and when I opened my bag, the money wasn't there. I was shocked and embarrassed, too."

"Some pickpocket might have laid hands on your money."

"That's not possible. I commuted by an auto rickshaw. Nobody came that close to me. Half of the shops hadn't even opened yet. There's no question of theft."

"Maybe it fell out of your purse, then."

"Come on, Sam! I had zipped the purse."

"Are you sure you took the money with you? You must check again in the cupboard."

"I have already checked. Sam, I think Sargam stole my money because she was the only one at home when I left for the market. Yesterday, when I had got my salary and kept it in the cupboard, she was there with me in my room."

"No, Shivi. You can't cast such a grave doubt."

"Sam, this is the second time it has happened. Last month also, I had kept my salary in the cupboard. When I retrieved the money after a few days, five thousand rupees were missing from the packet."

"Really? You didn't tell me!"

"Yes, I felt maybe I would have dropped the money somewhere, but now I know who took my money."

"Shivi, this is a sensitive matter, and you should not blame Sargam based on your reasoning."

"Sam, just think about it—how is Sargam able to manage her expenses? Where are funds for her out-station trips, weekend brunch with friends, and shopping coming from? How can so many expenses be covered by savings from the pocket money that you've been giving her?"

Sam didn't have an answer to that but told her to be vigilant, and the matter ended there.

A week later, at the annual meeting of Seva Troop, Sam came to know through one of his friends at the East Delhi branch that there were whispers in the office about

Ranjan receiving threats from the people with whom he was colluding earlier to get commissions. The grapevine had it that he had been siphoning off relief materials for money for a long time. However, due to recent changes in the organisational structure, he could not carry out his illegal activities. So, the gangs with whom he was coordinating had turned against him.

One day, shocking information poured in and stunned everyone at the office—Ranjan had been severely injured in a car crash and was in a critical state at a hospital. Within an hour, the news of his death also came in. Endless gossip began. The questions doing the rounds ranged from how it happened to whether it was actually an accident and whether there was a monetary dispute involved. Many suspected the involvement of gangs. There was a storm of questions and theories, but no evidence of how and why this had happened.

Ranjan's demise brought about some remarkable changes in the lives of Sam and Shivi. This development, coupled with the ouster of undeserving relatives of promoters from key managerial positions, opened up avenues for Sam's promotion. Shivi was also more comfortable, as the constant fear of Ranjan was no longer there. Their professional life took a positive turn, and things were now on the right track.

Meanwhile, Sargam's activities became more suspicious. At home, she offended Sam and Shivi openly. She stayed at her friend's place on weekends. She misbehaved with her mother too, and sounded irritated most of the time. This took a toll on Shivi's mental peace.

Sam tried to get things under control, but his effort went to waste, as Sargam seemed to be out of her mind. She stooped down to really low levels, cunningly accusing Shivi of having an extramarital affair. She claimed to have seen Shivi with a man at a cafe twice. Sam and Shivi had always stuck to open and honest communication. Their trust in each other was firm, and Sam disregarded Sargam's made-up stories. However, he was in no mood to tolerate Sargam's nonsense anymore. He allowed Shivi to handle it the way she wanted. Shivi stopped talking to Sargam. Sargam's mother forbade Sargam from speaking to Sam. In a sense, she isolated Sargam from Sam and Shivi. Though Shivi was looking to get some peace, a week of no contact with Sargam left her very disheartened. One evening, she was having a candid talk with Sam when she burst out crying and said, "Why did this happen? Why did Sargam try to malign my character?"

Sam consoled her and said, "Shivi, don't worry. It might just be a phase. She will realise her mistake, but you'll have to wait until it happens."

"I know that, but I can't understand why life can't be simple on all fronts at the same time."

"Don't ask for so much from life, Shivi. You just have to keep going with a pure heart. If she is getting swayed by emotions, she has to learn to correct her thought process."

"Sammy, she is in the wrong company. I'm sure of that. Someone is brainwashing her. Otherwise, why would she behave this way? I know we aren't the best of friends, but we're still sisters! I can't believe she went to such an extent just out of sibling rivalry. I hope she talks to me once again and things become normal. This phase is so tough."

Sam patted her head, and Shivi slept in his embrace.

Flowers convey a host of feelings

Through their fragrance.

Whilst the top notes

Are potent and entrancing

The base notes often hold

The whiff of their pain and tingling.

Chapter 16

Is It Time for Revelation?

A couple of months later, under the umbrella of starry lights, Shivi was cosying up to the warmth of the bonfire when Sam carefully handed her a cup of hot milk. Both Mrs. Singh and Mrs. Fernandes sat next to her, advising her not to dance too much. Sam said to Shivi, "You must take care of yourself and the tiny life that is growing inside you. Why do you forget you are going to be a mother soon?"

"Sammy, I didn't forget! I didn't even dance too much. I ran out of breath for a few seconds."

Mrs Singh said to her, "You have to be extra careful. You can't take it so lightly."

Shivi reassuringly gave her mother a hug and said, "Mom, your grandchild is safe! Do not worry. I'm going to take proper care. I was happy for Vivaan and Dhaani and could not stop myself from dancing with them."

Her mother caringly patted her head. Sam also sat with them, and they all sipped the hot cardamom-flavoured milk. Dhaani came to check on Shivi and asked, "What happened? Are you alright? If you are feeling cold, you must rest in the room."

"No, my dear. I'm enjoying it here. It's just that I needed to sit down for some time after the little dance moves that I did. This angel doesn't allow me to be active at all!"

Everyone laughed. Meanwhile, Vivaan had also left the dance floor and came to check on Shivi.

Shivi said to Dhaani and Vivaan, "It is your special day. You both must enjoy it. We've waited so long for you both to be married. Just enjoy the celebration. Don't worry about me."

Sam added, "It's your wedding reception, guys! Take care of all your guests. We are taking care of Shivi."

Vivaan jokingly replied, "I'm more concerned about my little buddy in there! Shivi, you better be careful."

Shivi grinned at Vivaan, and they all had a hearty laugh.

Vivaan and Dhaani, the newlyweds, then returned to the stage for pictures with their guests, and later, the cake-cutting ceremony took place.

Shivi had patched up with Sargam and returned to talking terms with her a month after their spat. Since the time Sargam came to know that Shivi and Sam were going to have a child, Sargam changed a little and began spending more time at her friend's place. She became reserved yet respectful towards her family. She didn't come for the celebration, although Dhaani and Vivaan had invited her.

A couple of months later, Sam and Shivi were blessed with a baby girl, who was a xerox copy of Shivi. Sargam was in Haryana at that time, as she had just started a job there.

Shivi had talked to Sargam over the phone and wanted her to meet the little one soon. Sargam also expressed her joy over the phone. Two days after their baby girl was born, Sargam's close friend visited Shivi and gave her an envelope that Sargam had sent. The rattle gave the hint that there was a piece of jewellery inside. Shivi thought it might be a gift for the child. She kept it safe, and after Sargam's friend went away, she opened it. Astounded at what she saw, she called Sam. He was equally surprised and took the piece of jewellery from her. It was Shivi's damaged gold bracelet that she had lost while fending off the beggar who had attacked her near the flyover years ago!

Along with the bracelet, there was a letter from Sargam.

Dear Shivi,

There is a lot that needs to be clarified—a lot of apologies that I owe. Believe me, I feel so embarrassed saying this—I was so wrong. I have been the culprit at so many points in your life. I feel pained as I say this, but my intentions for Sam weren't right. I was the one who was never happy with the two of you getting married. Throughout, I had been in touch with Ranjan despite your repeated warnings. I connived with him to create turmoil in your life, not realising that he was indeed a womaniser. My secret attraction towards Sam blinded my thinking abilities.

From the very beginning, Ranjan knew that I disregarded your guardianship. I feel that he also knew about my intentions for Sam. Ranjan indeed struck gold, as I followed whatever he said and wherever he led me. I never questioned his intent to break your marriage. All I wanted was for you to be out of Sam's life. Ranjan's immorality rubbed off on me, and I did not realise when it overpowered my reasoning ability. Despite corrective efforts from all of you, I never saw the reality. I have brought shame to Mummy too, and I can only ask for forgiveness with every breath now.

Falling into Ranjan's trap was quick because I couldn't decipher my feelings for Sam and classified them wrongly. Then it was just a matter of seeing what I wanted to see and hearing only what I wanted to hear. I don't have the courage to face you both now and won't ever have it in this life, to say the least.

You might wonder how this realisation came about! Let me shed some light on it because you deserve to know about it more than anyone else.

When Ranjan passed away in the car accident, I was called by the police, as my phone number was on his phone's last dialled list. They then connected with his brother in Europe. After his consent, they handed over some of his belongings to me. His brother had said that he'll come to Delhi in six months' time. He requested that I keep the house keys with me until then. Since Ranjan didn't have any other family members, I went to his apartment to keep those belongings there. There was a locker in his cupboard, which used to be locked always—at least whenever I visited him. But on this day, it was open. His clothes were also falling out, so I thought of putting the stuff back in. What I found in that locker changed my whole life. I can't even mention some things here! In that mess, I found this broken bracelet of yours. I immediately recognised it. My hands began trembling. At that very moment, I understood what Ranjan had been hiding from me. He had been fooling me about his *pure* intentions for you. I began reading his diary, and the ground slipped from below my feet. He always wanted you to be with him and not with Sam. You judged him rightly. He also had a few bones to pick with Sam, and all he wanted to do was destroy Sam's career.

I still cannot blame it all on Ranjan. There are some more truths that you need to know. It was Ranjan who ensured that the management didn't approve your leave applications for your wedding. However, it was me who revealed your wedding plans to him. I even tried to discourage Mummy from getting you married to Sam. However, I guess she figured out my intention. She never mentioned anything openly, but she guarded your and Sam's relationship from my evil intentions. I never wanted to move in with Mummy because I wanted to stay around him. I even lied about getting a job. I used to go to East Delhi to meet Ranjan every day at the office. He had promised me he'd get me a job. When Ranjan was in trouble and had asked me for monetary help, I stole money from your purse. However, I wasn't aware that he had connections with anti-social elements who were demanding money from him. I got to know about it only after I read his diary.

Cutting a long story short, I have terribly failed as a sister and shall spend the rest of my life rectifying my follies. However, I am purposely going away from all of you now. I had a job offer from a company in Delhi too, but I declined it. I am moving to an undisclosed location to live a life of repentance. If ever I feel that my repentance is over, I shall meet you all again. Till then, please forgive me if you can.

With love,

Sargam.

Shivi cried on reading the letter, and Sam also had tears in his eyes. While hugging Sam, she said, "I can't believe all this. Why did she do this?"

She was out of breath and numb. Sam patted her and said, "Shivi, calm down. We shall trace her soon."

"Sammy, she should have talked to us."

"I know—she should have! Perhaps she was embarrassed beyond a limit and couldn't face us."

Despite there being no way of getting in touch with Sargam, Shivi and her family tried a lot to find her. Her friends also didn't answer the family's calls. After a month of relentless tries, Mrs Singh told them that they must accept Sargam's choice, as she would need time to overcome her grief and the massive guilt.

A few days later, the family fixed the date for the newborn's naming ceremony. They hadn't been able to connect with Sargam until now. Shivi wanted to wait until Sargam returned, but they couldn't have delayed the ceremony any further. They named the baby *Swara* at a temple with the blessings of Mrs. Singh and Mrs. Fernandes. Just as the naming ceremony was completed,

Shivi spotted Sargam standing at the gate of the temple. Sargam's friend had convinced her and brought her along. It was an intensely emotional moment. Holding her baby tightly, Shivi ran towards Sargam. Sargam knelt down penitently. Shivi also sat on the ground in front of her. She made Sargam hold the tiny child and wiped away her tears. Then Sam approached the sisters. He patted Sargam's head caringly and took them all inside the temple. It was as if Sargam's apologies needed no words today, as her mother also hugged her at once. Joy again spread its wings amongst them as little Swara giggled and responded to everyone's cuddles.

Repentance is the way

A soul gets a burden off the chest.

Especially so after realisation,

Self-test, and retest.

Compassionate understanding

Can make or break relationships

In this world—here—and

It can also bring out the best!

www.ingramcontent.com/pod-product-compliance
Lightning Source LLC
Chambersburg PA
CBHW060538160726
47991CB00001B/379